LAKESIDE HIDEAWAY

Noelene Jenkinson

Chapter 1

Billie Gibbs sped in her blue SUV along the bush road of the Grampians foothills leading back to the main road, happily delayed by helping school friend, Piper Thorne, recover a vital old family art relic from thieves who had stolen it years before.

She had left Melbourne days ago, intending to drive directly to the lake shack and disappear for a while but fate had intervened. On reflection, a welcome accidental interruption to her much needed escape. It made her pause to draw breath, slowed the pace of her life and created a distraction from the emotional anguish in which she had hastily left the city.

Billie turned left onto the Western Highway but instead of heading straight to Reedy Lake on the outskirts of Horsham, she was driven by some nagging intuition to pull off when she reached the Coach Roadhouse again. Waitress, Holly Duncan, had captured her attention earlier, a lost soul, perhaps craving friendship and clearly troubled. Not so much unhappy as uneasy within herself. Why this seemed important, Billie had no idea but she could spare five minutes to grab a coffee and a quick word with her.

All she vaguely remembered from the news five years ago was that Holly's mother had gone missing in the area while driving through. The Coach Roadhouse had been the woman's last stop and no trace of her had ever been found. At least not that Billie had heard about. But then, these days, she was a reluctant visitor home to family in the Wimmera. Which shot her with a sense of guilt as she recalled Holly's comment earlier that day about the importance of keeping in touch with family.

Apparently, soon after her mother's fruitless search had wound down, Holly had returned to the district, living and working with owners, Sid and Gracie Townsend, at the roadhouse. Billie idly wondered if the investigation was still open or the paperwork shelved in a forgotten box in some obscure basement file room. Unresolved and labelled a cold case unless new information came to light when it would be reopened.

As Billie parked and strode across the car park into the restaurant, she was pleased to see Holly still on duty. She noticed the good looking driver who had been a source of self-conscious attraction for the girl and his B-Double truck had long gone.

Approaching the counter, Holly caught her eye and came over, her initial smile fading. 'Hey, Billie.' She leaned forward and lowered her voice. 'Did you find Piper's boyfriend? Is he okay?'

Billie beamed. 'Yes. Everything's great. How about you? Get the chance of a few words with that hunk of a truckie?'

Holly flushed but knew exactly who she meant. 'Oh, you mean Tom Searle? He often passes through.'

She knew him well enough to know his name but he was clearly a regular. 'Handy.'

'Oh,' she scoffed, waving an arm, 'blokes like that don't take any notice of the staff here. They order, eat and leave. Straight back up into their rigs and out onto that highway again.'

'You should chat him up next time.'

'Guys like that are always on the move. Their poor wives must never see them.'

'Well he sure looked the goods. There was a lot to like about that body.'

Holly grinned. 'Did you want to order?'

'A soy cappuccino to go, thanks, Holly.' When her drink was ready, she said, 'I'm heading out to an old shack on Reedy Lake. Do you know it?'

Holly nodded. 'Yeah. Sid goes fishing out there sometimes. Not so much this time of year.'

Billie shrugged. 'If you get a day off, you're welcome to come out for a visit. It's at the northern end. My friend, Sasha Lowe's family own the property and she offered it to me for a few weeks. Said no one goes there much in winter so it should be peaceful and quiet.'

Holly studied her for a while. 'I'll keep it in mind.'

Billie grabbed a table napkin from a holder on the counter and jotted down her mobile number. Handing it over, she said, 'Give me a call if you decide to come.'

Holly accepted it. 'Are you sure? Sounds like you're up here for a personal break.'

'In a few days, I'll probably be glad of the company,' Billie joked, knowing she was far from over her matters of the heart and that, once she was alone, the reality of her situation would probably hit home with force.

Leaving the roadhouse after talking to Holly and driving on to Reedy Lake, Billie thought about the amazing events of recent days. Speeding away from her fiancé in Melbourne, having no idea what direction to take but finding herself winding along the coastal Great Ocean Road then inland through the lush green countryside of the Western District to Hamilton and, finally, the small southern mountains village of Dunkeld.

Which is where the disruption had started.

She cringed to recall she hadn't been either friendly or gracious when she saw her former school friend, Piper Thorne, in the town's main street. At that point, having hurriedly packed up and rushed from the city in a daze, the highly-charged emotional reason she left was still firmly lodged in her mind.

But after their brief chat of re-acquaintance, Billie's nervous tension had eased and she felt more agreeable. Which prompted her decision to stay on a few nights, languishing over sleep-ins to avoid facing the world but forced to go out and eat. Which meant strolling the quiet tourist streets of the town, greeted warmly by locals. It was a calming and reassuring interval. Random, but, as she discovered, worth the pause.

Because when Piper reappeared in Dunkeld earlier today as she was about to leave for the lake, clamped a fixed gaze on her from across the street again, explained her dilemma and pleaded for her help, a torrent of rage had exploded inside Billie. Honestly? Some callous self-indulgent individuals thought they could get away with cheating without any consideration for the damage and consequences that followed.

So she had snapped. The Davids of this world needed to be stopped. Which meant she found herself offering to help and becoming engrossed in Piper's quest for reckoning in her family. Ending in one exciting and action-packed afternoon.

Still on a high and needing coffee, strangely wanting to touch base with Holly again, she had stopped at the highway roadhouse. Not easily embarking on new friendships from a disorderly family upbringing, Billie sensed a kindred spirit in Holly Duncan. She felt curious about the attractive roadhouse waitress and her heartbreaking personal background. Another whose life had not easily flowed, revealing a deep sense of insecurity. She genuinely hoped Holly dropped by at the lake some time.

Even as her destination entered her thoughts, Billie discovered she was approaching the turn off to the gravelled road across a paddock to the cabin, such as it was. Peering through the windscreen, Billie admitted she thought the old hut might have fallen down by now. It was fairly basic even back in the day, but, nope, as the light bushland thinned ahead, she noticed it was still there in all its humble rustic glory.

Billie pulled her SUV to a stop under a carport at the side of the building. Out front, pale sunlight glinted on the glassy surface of the lake. She wondered if coming out here by herself had been such a good idea after all. Water birds, animals and critters were going about their business. But not another human in sight, although apparently it was a great fishing spot.

Billie grabbed her suitcase and wandered to explore her accommodation for the next week or two, or however long she needed to stay to kick her mental chaos. She paused on the small deck outside the front door and took in her view.

Wow, all this for free. Tourists paid a fortune for such stunning tranquil views. The broad expanse of fresh water stretched for about a kilometre to Willow Bend, a distant headland that extended into the lake, leading to the farthest part beyond sight. Light eucalyptus bushland and occasional banks of high reeds hugged its edges.

Compared to a noisy city it sure was quiet and isolated but then Sasha had assured her no one was likely to visit. She would hardly see a soul. Have absolute privacy.

Even though, once Billie's mind was made up, she had left Melbourne in a hurry, she had at least some sense of mind to grab a handful of novels to read and her laptop, hoping she could charge her mobile phone compliments of the old single wire power line that she noticed tracking across the paddock from the distant Lowe farmhouse on the property.

Still packed with plenty of supplies from Dunkeld, thoughts of Horsham and her parents briefly flitted across her mind but she pushed them aside. Not now. Not today. Maybe a personal visit to check on her mother just the once but that would be it. This break was sorely needed time out and she intended to be selfish with it. Pull back. Think. Analyse, but not too much. That might prove even more depressing.

Turning to greet her new temporary lodgings, Billie smiled. Sasha had been right. The old timber shack wasn't fancy but the stack of firewood against the wall to the far side of the central front door looked promising. It was a long time since she had lit an open fire. Billie only hoped there was also plenty of water in the tank she had passed around the side of the shack. And she crossed her fingers there was at least a half comfortable bed somewhere inside.

Apparently this little lakeside hideaway was never locked so she tried the rusty knob with her free hand, relieved when it turned and the door squeaked open. It needed a push with her shoulder but she was in.

With the full length front window blinds down, the one large main room was dim but spread across the front of the shack. A compact kitchenette with a gas stove, sink and bar fridge together with a small square table and two chairs appeared adequate enough at one end. A small sofa and a big old arm chair were grouped around an awesome open fireplace at the other end. She would need to work out how to get that started for warmth soon.

Billie noticed there was no television but that wasn't an issue. She worked long hours and never watched it anyway. She and David shared a busy social life. Billie caught her breath. *Used to share* a busy social life. In fact, any life together. But that was all over now. In the past. This getaway was the groundwork for a new beginning.

Dumping her case, Billie pulled up the shades and light flooded in. Along with the views. She just stood and gaped. Seated cosily inside or out sprawled in a chair on a fine day, she would have an uninterrupted private view of the lake. Perfect. Everyone should have a little escape place like this. To emotionally debrief, question your life or, in her case, heal wounds. It was basic but it was only two weeks. She would deal.

First things first. Taking up her case again, she wandered through the one door to the back of the shack. Two good sized bedrooms with a separate toilet and bathroom between led off a narrow hallway. Sasha had told her the toilet was a septic system. Billie didn't care. This was the bush after all. She merely hoped that it worked.

Since her free bed and board was covered in a fine film of dust, clearly no one had been here for quite a while. So she changed clothes and set to work with a broom and dustpan, and a damp cloth. Then she scrubbed the small kitchen area and table, cleaned out the fridge, stowed the food from her esky and took the sofa cushions outside for a decent thumping that released a powdery cloud before replacing them again.

Later, opening all the doors and rummaging around in the one double storage cupboard, to her delight – obviously small things were going to easily amuse her out here – she found two very comfortable padded folding deck chairs. She leant one against a wall near the door, deciding it was prudent to keep it inside in this weather when she wasn't using it. But close handy on a sunny day when she would set it up outside.

With daylight fading early this time of year, Billie planted her hands on her hips and eyed the coals and ash in the fireplace. This would test her skills but she found piles of old newspapers and a bucket of kindling kindly left by whoever had camped here last. Not recently that was for sure.

Soon the warmth of the first licking flames proved she hadn't forgotten the basics of lighting a fire and cheered her mood.

There would be no fancy restaurant meals out here, not like in the city where it had been taken for granted every other evening, so she set to work boiling rice and steaming vegetables, slicing off a chunk of bread from a bakery loaf she bought in Dunkeld early this morning. She piled the stir-fry onto a plate, grabbed a fork from the cutlery drawer and sank onto the sofa by the fire to eat.

Tired and comfortable, hugging a hot mug of tea, Billie became aware that her days would be all like this so she had better keep her mind occupied, her thoughts positive and, most importantly, not become a couch potato and get some exercise. Back in Melbourne, that meant hitting the gym. Not out here. The country awaited. Bush tracks led everywhere so she would just follow them and see where they led. She had her bearings out here and knew her directions so it was unlikely she would get lost.

Although the clock on her mobile told her it was still early, after the emotional upheaval of the last week and today's hectic turn helping Piper and her family, Billie scrambled into pyjamas and groaned with pleasure to snuggle beneath a doona, welcoming sleep.

She woke when it was barely daylight, stretched and reluctantly pushed back the bed covers to tiptoe out and check the fire. A few low coals still glowed so she nursed them back to life. Once it was crackling, she braved a quick lukewarm shower, keeping to the rules on the bathroom notice advising a strict five minute limit to save tank water.

After pulling up the blinds, breakfast was cereal in a bowl and a mug of coffee curled up before her companion open fire. Now what, Billie wondered, as she rinsed her dishes in the sink?

The day promised to be cold but fine so she braved a short stint outdoors on the deck chair with a rug from her bedroom wrapped around her for extra warmth. She watched small ducks playing in and around the reeds for a while. Rosellas and shrieking lorikeets flew between the gum trees. A small group of pelicans flew in to gently land and serenely sail about.

They managed to appear content, Billie

thought. She must work on that while she was here. And wasn't that the purpose? Deal with the sudden disruption to her life. Although only weeks since the split, already Billie acknowledged her changed life situation. Now it was all about a new direction and what she wanted that to look like. Plenty of food for thought. Decisions to be made. The reason she was here. Next time around, if she ever braved another relationship, she would proceed with caution.

For now, she would regard this isolated setting of nature not as the opponent but as a friend to restore some semblance of peace to her mind. An ally in restoring balance again.

The next day took on a similar routine to the first. Bird and wildlife watching, becoming acquainted with their habits. Sleeping, waking, eating and a stroll into the bush. Picking sprays of early wattle to display in an old glass jar she found in the kitchen cupboard along with candles she lit, sticking them onto saucers with the wax drippings, to add a bit more ambience than the dim single light bulb in the ceiling.

By late afternoon she even opened a novel. A spooky crime thriller which was probably not the best idea out here. She could have sunk into a pit of gloom. Stayed in her pyjamas and not bothered to get dressed. Not like she would be expecting visitors any time soon. Unless Holly contacted her and showed up. Right about now a few hours of female company over a bottle of wine would be welcome.

The bouts of idle contemplation did serve some purpose. Billie gradually faced the vast differences between the city life she had come to know and embrace with her high-powered accountancy position, the modern city apartment she had shared with her fiancé – *ex-fiancé* she reminded herself - compared to growing up in this Wimmera countryside. And how she now passed her days out here in the bush shack forcing everything to slow down.

The attacks of unwanted heartache that gripped her body when they struck and the simple peace and beauty by the water in this natural setting felt incompatible.

Yet revealed how much she had allowed a focus on being busy and acquiring material *things* to enter her life. When you got right down to it, out here in this simple excuse for a hut, what existed was all she needed. Not so much stuff. It hadn't been wrong so much as an influenced conversion from friends and work colleagues around her.

Friends, Billie thought bitterly. You couldn't always trust those either. Smiling and lying to your face while deceiving behind your back.

Okay, she pulled herself up short. She would allow herself five minutes to indulge in self-pity. Get the waterworks and recriminations over, then take herself in hand, start thinking about what happens next. The fact that at this particular unhappy moment she had no idea what that step would be didn't help but didn't matter. Something would crop up. As crazy and spiritual as it sounded, she had to believe that. It was far less effort and wear on the nerves to not think and plan all the time, just let her future evolve as it surely would.

That night, perhaps because of David's constant annoying phone calls and texts, all unanswered, and distracted by her churning mind of recent days, to her annoyance Billie tossed and turned, unable to sleep. Puzzling why he bothered when it was his decision to separate. She didn't fight it. In desperation, she turned her phone to silent, shrugged the rug around her and strolled outside onto the deck to practise deep breathing and simply being still. The winter night was icy cold, utterly silent and calm. She stared out over the lake, fascinated by the simplicity of a shining half-moon spreading a glaze across the surface.

She stayed until her limbs began to grow numb and she shivered, returning indoors and under the doona again, immediately sinking into a sound sleep.

Only to have the silence shattered too early next morning by the sound of a plane flying low and close. Billie sat up in bed, frowning. There was no airport near here.

She shuffled sleepily out onto the deck,

hugging a thick jacket around her pyjamas, shielding her eyes from the early morning sun to investigate but didn't see anything. Some of the waterbirds had taken flight. Still hearing droning in the distance the other side of Willow Bend but no sight of an aircraft, she wondered if it was an emergency or in trouble and intended landing in a paddock.

She yawned and returned indoors. At least it was a bit of action although at this hour of the day not particularly welcome but unusual all the same.

Chapter 2

Clearly, one interruption today to her country serenity was not going to be enough. Soon after breakfast, Billie heard a vehicle approaching the shack from the paddock road. As it came closer, she peered through the small side window at the end of the hallway to see a battered white ute pull up alongside her SUV on the other side of the carport.

The man that unfolded himself from behind the wheel looked vaguely familiar. A local and, judging by the shabby jeans, checked shirt collar under a well-worn windcheater and muddy boots, probably a farmer. Billie frowned, still unable to place him.

He closed the ute door, pushed on a pair of aviator shades and stood a while staring out across the lake before turning a steady gaze in her direction. Caught. Embarrassing. Billie pulled away from the window, strode back through the shack and outside. By then, her visitor had reached the deck.

There was something else about him. The confident attitude. Toned muscled legs straining inside those tight old denims suggested something more than a bloke who worked out. She was annoyed no name came to mind. Even behind those glasses, she sensed his eyes travelled all over her, up and down. Not so much assessing her as a person or even a woman but more like watchful, like he was used to being on his guard.

After a moment's hesitation, one corner of his mouth tilted ever so slightly into the hint of a grin. He recognised her?

Billie's irritation rose. She hated being at a disadvantage.

'Sibilla Gibbs,' he drawled, surprised, removing his shades and hooking them into the top of his windcheater.

She raised her eyebrows. Few people knew her full name let alone used it anymore. Maybe only her mother. 'Billie.'

She thought back. Someone from school days? And then it came to her. The Sutton boy! The younger of the two brothers but he had been some years ahead of her in secondary. Wow, he'd grown into one impressive male.

'Noah?'

His eyes sparkled with humour that she still wasn't sure she had identified him correctly. 'It took a while.'

'It's *been* a while.' So, if memory served her correctly, the Sutton place joined the Lowe property. Which meant he was a neighbour and might have seen her arrive two days ago.

'Came to investigate the smoke from the chimney.'

'You must have needed binoculars for that.'

'Deserted places like this,' he nodded toward the shack, 'can get intruders and squatters. Being a neighbour, I usually keep an eye on the place.'

Great! He would be dutifully calling around to check on her?

'You know this is private property.'

Billie folded her arms. 'And you would know that I already know that.'

'Lowe's aware you're here?'

'Of course,' she scoffed and challenged, 'I can phone Sasha if you like.'

'No need. Out here, a female on your own, you need to be careful. Even this short distance from town is more remote than it seems.'

'That's exactly why I came. You know I grew up around here. I haven't forgotten my roots.'

He shrugged. 'I'm used to keeping people safe. Force of habit.'

That's right, he was a military man. Explained his take charge air of control. 'There's absolutely no reason for you to give a damn, Noah. I'm perfectly capable of taking care of myself.'

'Might be wise to rethink how long you stay and leave sooner.'

Billie scoffed 'No way. I just got here. I came

for a -' she faltered over the right word, 'break and I intend to see it through.'

'From work and the city?'

Billie felt no need to answer or explain. Instead, she ignored his probe and said, 'Thanks for stopping by.'

Noah seemed in no rush to leave. His gaze travelled over the shack. 'I come over here fishing occasionally. Place doesn't change much.'

Billie shrugged. 'Hasn't inside either.'

'You don't mind the discomfort?'

'Obviously not.' annoyed that she felt obliged since Noah wasn't moving Billie found some manners. Drawing on the custom of country hospitality and against her better judgement, she invited him in for a cuppa which – no surprise - he readily accepted. Once they were seated on the sofa by the fire, she mentioned the plane activity this morning.

'It was early, soon after sunrise. Woke me and, by the sound of it, half the ducks on the lake as well. Sasha promised me peace which I'm just beginning to appreciate.' Billie quipped. 'Did you hear it from your place?'

Noah didn't immediately reply. Sipped his coffee first before saying, 'Not from my farm, no.'

'Well, thinking more about it, now I'm growing curious. Only place to land around here is in the middle of a paddock.'

'It's possible it might have set down on a

local farm.'

'But that would be Lowe property on the east side of the lake. As far as I know, they don't have an airstrip. And it's unlikely to be aerial crop spraying, right? That's uncommon these days. Farmers use a boom spray behind a tractor.'

Noah remained vague and unconcerned. 'True. There's been no news or report of a crash landing so all must be well. It might have landed further out than you think or been sweeping low on some kind of property check,' he brushed aside her concerns.

Maybe she *was* making something out of nothing, Billie reasoned, and Noah was right. After all, she hadn't even seen the plane, simply heard it in the distance. She had probably blown a moment's entertainment out of proportion to its importance.

Noah was drilling her with that intense stare again. 'So, you're not staying with the folks while you're home?'

None of his business and his smooth change of topic from the plane didn't pass unnoticed. 'Not this time.' Or ever.

'If I recall you come from a big family in the Gibbs clan.'

Billie shrugged. 'You have a good memory. I'm the middle kid of seven.'

'I see your oldest brother and a couple of your sisters around town.'

'The only ones who stayed.' Preferring to cut the family conversation short, she changed the subject. 'What about your family? Heard from my youngest sister, Meredith, that your parents died a few years back.'

Noah nodded. 'Yeah.'

'Sorry to hear that. It must have been difficult, especially when your brother was killed so tragically young all those years ago, too.' When Noah fell silent, his expression blank, Billie shrugged, 'I imagine it's hard with all your family gone, returning to an empty farm,' she said softly. 'Being the only one left, I mean,' she trailed off awkwardly.

He didn't acknowledge her uttered sympathy. 'I have my dog Buddy to keep me company and plenty of visitors.'

Catching his shadowed glance, Billie thought, *Okay, touchy subject. Moving on.* 'You were in the defence forces, weren't you?'

Noah nodded. 'Joined up straight out of high school. After ten years, I kinda longed to get back to the country. It was time.'

'Most of us can't wait to leave.' She hesitated, 'So, you're not married or-?'

'Divorced.'

The blunt tone in his voice and hunching of shoulders suggested a whole other story there. For another time. Not that she needed to know or expected to see him around. But he seemed a nice enough bloke, if guarded. A ruggedly handsome older version of the good looking school boy she recalled.

'What about you?' He glanced down at her hand. 'No rings. A partner?'

Surprised by his quiet question, Billie slid her glance away from him, out the window and across the lake. 'I was engaged. Once.'

Recently. Relationships were fragile matters she had discovered. So easily snapped off sharp and quick like a twig.

'I guess you'll be catching up with the folks while you're home.'

Billie felt bad. Since Noah was a lone adult, her response would probably disappoint him. His family had been hard working farmers, middle class and respectable. Billie's experience was tarnished with the reality of having been one of a large tribe of siblings. A product of a loud-mouthed, heavy-handed father and an overwhelmed mother who woke each day to a mountain of work and a compliant attitude merely for survival.

'I guess I'll make contact with my mother at some point. Make sure she's as okay as she can be under the circumstances. Last I heard, my parents Heather and Jack are on welfare, still together and living in the same old rundown house.'

Noah raised his eyebrows. 'You've been kept informed.'

'My sister, Meredith, keeps in touch. I'm not

so heartless that I would write them off. At least, not my mother. You can't help but admire such unjustified endurance staying in a hard marriage. The weak need support and I will always be there for her.'

Noah eyed her with drilled intent, considering her personal perspective and probably knowing the depth of her tough family situation. A lot was gossip but much of it was not far from the truth. Tired of covering up, making excuses or playing down her family disrepute around town, she decided to be honest and blunt.

'Considering what each Gibbs child had to work with, it's a credit to most of us that we made something of our lives. It could have been worse. None of us might have crawled out of our hole. Now *that* would have been a disaster.

'Apparently Johnny is still free with his fists. Brady and Danny were wise to get out when they did. I haven't seen them in years but I understand they're somewhere up north working on outback stations. Courtney and Brittany chose to be eye candy and stay local. They have blokes and kids now but no rings on their fingers. No security.'

She could talk. She *did* have a ring and look how that turned out.

Noah processed her version of the family before responding. 'What's your own story?'

Billie tossed him a wry smile. 'I gritted my

teeth. Learned self-defence, chose my battles to keep the peace. But I always had a plan in mind. Escape, an education and a career.

'While she was growing up and before I left, I took our youngest sister, Meredith, under my wing. Loaded her with encouragement. Taught her to think smart. My protégé is a barrister now,' Billie couldn't help but proudly boast. 'Man, you should see that young woman strut her stuff in a courtroom with poise and style. I've watched her in action. She sure looks good in a tailored suit.'

'We each find our own path in life,' Noah said quietly. 'Even if it's not always what we expect.'

He rose to leave so Billie stood, too. As he passed her closely and their shoulders brushed, she felt a deep sense of awareness, smelling the earthy goodness that surrounded him. Noah didn't hesitate and obviously felt nothing.

Outside on the deck, he paused. 'Take care out here. Best to stay up this end of the lake.'

Billie frowned over what sounded more like a warning than concerned advice. Strange. 'I don't plan on going far.' Even if she was, she wasn't about to tell him and she'd do it of her own choice without his permission.

As he slipped his shades back on again, turned and strode away, his boots thumping across the deck, Billie sized him up from behind. Thick sandy hair, long easy strides. She wasn't quite sure what to make of Farmer Sutton. If she was honest, visually, he was the goods. A strong reliable man any woman would clamour to snag. But he was a remote individual. Independent like her. Maybe seeing action overseas in the service had something to do with it.

Either way, she had no interest in any man any time soon. Lesson learned. Staying single and free was starting to look appealing. She might even make it permanent.

But now that Noah Sutton had paid her a visit, virtually commanding she stay at the shack like a prisoner with that serious directive tone of his, she wondered if a little walk of exploration might not be in order. His cautious reaction niggled her inquisitive mind.

In her city office, she was used to delving deep, following money and grappling with figures. Working out problems. So she was willing to bet there was more to that plane than Sutton would share. If it was harmless, why not? His evasion sparked her obstinate streak.

While he might be a local and know what he was talking about, she was convinced Noah knew something. Every time she dashed out onto the deck for a glimpse of it, she could only hear it beyond Willow Bend and the trees. Only way to find out what was happening down there was on foot.

Or by water. She had noticed a small row boat tied up half hidden in the reeds at the end of the deck and promised herself on a milder day she would give it a spin.

The entire east side of the lake was Lowe property so, technically, she wouldn't be trespassing. But really, out here in this lightly-timbered bushland? Who would see or know? Apart from the one who had just left, she hadn't seen or heard another human being since her arrival.

Billie lasted another two days, anchored to the shack and its surrounds. The first day, opening the blinds to barely daylight, a light misty fog hugged the surface of the still water. She figured no small plane without radar would be flying in this weather.

She braved the outdoor chill for a long walk out onto the track leading across the paddock, through the always-open rusty gate to the main road and back again. A few wispy drifts of fog still lingered on the lake's surface but the day opened up and the sun briefly came out, so she soaked up its feeble warmth on the deck in the early afternoon. When clouds gathered and darkened, the wind picked up driving her indoors again.

For an entire day yesterday, the fine weather had worsened with heavy soaking showers pushing through. Forcing her to actually open up one of her novels and delve into its story. Eating and drinking too much tea and coffee, continually feeding the fire, watching her wood pile dwindle.

But since Noah's visit, Billie's curiosity increased about the activity beyond Willow Bend. After the foggy morning two days ago and rain yesterday, she played a hunch that, with an improvement in the weather and regularly passing overhead, the plane just might be back this morning.

So without breakfast or her usual first mug of coffee to see her through, Billie scrambled out of her warm bed, rugged up in warm clothes, sneakers and a beanie and decided to investigate the recurring little local mystery that had cropped up nearby.

During those first days when she heard the plane overhead, Billie was mildly annoyed to be rudely woken far too early. Just when she was starting to enjoy sleep-ins instead of her usual city routine of waking to an alarm, a commute and the prospect of another working day. Besides, the more she slept, the less she thought about that nasty cheating piece of work she had left behind.

Now, she didn't really care that her peace and quiet were interrupted because the plane was buzzing around almost every other day. That in itself was odd and baffling, spiking her interest.

She jogged off around the east side of the lake which bordered the Lowe family property.

Water birds rustled among the thick borders of reeds at the lake's verges, her racing strides following a lightly trodden pathway winding in and out of eucalypt bushland lit by weak early daylight as the sun was about to crack the horizon.

Growing up around here in the country, she remembered often jumping onto one of the few bikes belonging to her siblings if there was any event or new place to investigate when the attraction for their favourites dwindled. Especially in the summer holidays when it was too hot to walk and quicker to ride.

So it seemed natural for Billie to head off exploring to satisfy the questions raised in her mind, even though Noah had brushed them off. With a sense of adventure, but also caution, because instinct told her it was definitely unusual that planes would be out here so often in this quiet sheltered place.

After steady running, her legs began to complain. At the same time as the headland jutting out to Willow Bend loomed ahead, a familiar sound soon lifted her spirits and her pace increased. Nailed it! Her heart pounded with excitement.

Heading off the track, crouching low alongside the water, using the cover of trees and undergrowth damp with dewy moisture, Billie was in full sight of the small campground area near the jetty and the other half of the lake.

She kept her distance and turned her gaze skyward, scanning the clear blue, the plane engine growing louder. She waited until it came into view, slowly descending toward the lake. At first she thought it was going to ditch and wondered why the pilot hadn't aimed for an open paddock. There were plenty of those around out here. Then she realised it had no wheels underneath but a set of floats either side instead.

That's why the plane was always so close! It would be landing on the water! It gradually descended with gentle precision and skimmed onto the lake, turning to motor slowly toward the nearby jetty.

Until it landed, Billie hadn't noticed any people or activity but the moment the small aircraft was down, vehicles and manpower appeared from two directions. Oddly, the pilot remained in the plane while the four blokes on the ground tied it up and began unloading boxes and packages, transferring them into the back of the two covered utes and a black four wheel drive. Supplies of some kind, she wondered, watching with interest but careful to remain still and concealed.

One of the men suddenly spun in her direction, produced a handgun, stood still and stared. That weapon wasn't legal and he was handling it as though needing it for self-defence. From who, way out here? It certainly wasn't a farming rifle or sport, for which he might have a licence. Billie narrowed her gaze and froze, hardly daring to breathe or move. He looked vaguely familiar. She was a local and this guy could be too. But, for the moment, she couldn't put a name to the face.

The whole delivery and cargo transfer was over within ten minutes. After untying the plane, one man dashed in off the jetty and they all started piling back into the utes. Thinking it was safe, Billie stood up, believing she was hidden behind a tree trunk.

Perhaps it was her movement or she made a noise because the same man as before who was about to step into the four wheel drive, turned in her direction. She edged further behind the tree, lowered herself to the ground and crawled toward the reeds. Just in case. If she heard footsteps approach, she could slide into the water and hide. Ducks did it all the time.

For terrifying long moments, she closed her eyes and waited.

Billie heard rustling close. A voice further away growled low, 'See anything?'

Another responded with impatient muttering.

Finally, she heard the vehicle doors slam, engines kick into life and roar away. Her whole body sank with relief but her mind was still wired with adrenalin and when she tried to stand, her legs were weak and shaking. She gave herself a moment to recover. Meanwhile, the float plane had drifted from the jetty before its engine spluttered into life again too. Billie watched it speed up and take off.

Hands on hips staring after it, Billie shook her head and frowned in amazement. Strange. Definitely suspicious. What goods needed such speed and a sense of secrecy? One answer sprang to mind. In fact, considering the sense of urgency she witnessed from the entire short operation, it was highly probably and likely.

Billie wished she could have crept closer to read the number plate on the black four wheel drive. The local policeman, Ewan Holt, would have been able to check it and see who was involved. Which, for now anyway, was pointless because she had no proof of anything.

Not sure she had the energy for the return hike, Billie took one step at a time. For the entire return trek, her mind buzzed on replay with every detail of what she had just seen.

The whole episode reeked of dishonesty. Out here, people stopped to yarn. If the pilot and vehicle drivers knew each other, the pilot would have stepped out, lit a smoke and taken the time for a chat. Not to mention the man springing to alert, his gaze channelled in her direction.

Any local bloke might have glanced her way, made a joke or cajoled a mate to go check it out. And certainly wouldn't be packing a firearm. Not the man in the four wheel drive. In the brief glimpse she caught of him, his whole stance spoke fear of discovery. If he had been unafraid and legal, he would hardly have turned a hair.

Eventually she made it back to the shack. In the tiny kitchenette, Billie was suddenly unaccountably energetic and ravenous. This morning's leftover adrenaline rush? As she scrambled eggs, fried tomatoes and made toast while the kettle boiled for another mug of tea, she realised that for the entire two-hour experience, she hadn't thought about David for a single moment. All her energy and attention had been directed elsewhere.

Billie cringed with annoyance that any thoughts about her ex-fiancé and the blatant cheek of what he had done could infiltrate her mind without the slightest encouragement.

Some nights were restless, and not all her days since the break were good or easy but she was surviving. Clearly, her emotional recovery was going to take a while but Billie felt strongly and positive that at least it was underway.

And she believed, disregarding strange planes and a cute neighbour, she had this lakeside hideaway to thank for that.

Chapter 3

That afternoon, Billie sat out on the deck trying to read but finding herself continually distracted by the antics of the water birds out on the lake and splashing among the nearby reeds. Even a kookaburra, sending out its noisy laugh to echo through the bush, momentarily diverted her attention.

So when a faint high-pitched buzzing sounded overhead, Billie frowned and listened. With a light winter wind gently drifting in her direction from the south, the faint humming carried to her over the water. Ducks began to suddenly take flight. Shading her eyes and squinting into the pale afternoon sun, she eventually made out the tiny outline of a drone hovering at height a short distance out over the lake.

If she had been inside, she would never have heard or noticed it. Billie wasn't sure if that was a good or bad thing.

Someone had to be operating the controls within sight, keeping track of their remote machine, but Billie's intense gaze around the natural bushland right down to the water's edges revealed nothing.

She grew troubled that she couldn't see the operator to know who was in control. Right now, they could probably see her but she couldn't see them.

It was a weekday so kids should be at school. A local photographer maybe? A new owner trying it out on a test run? She knew those contraptions often had a feedback camera and took photos. Out here, Billie felt invaded yet again and more than mildly concerned.

Was it mere coincidence that it was near the shack where she expected peace and privacy? Neither of which she was so far easily achieving. And, as her mind churned over, that it should appear on the same day she had spotted the plane activity at Willow Bend?

She sighed in frustration. It could be someone quite innocently operating the device.

Or not.

Rubbing her arms against a nasty sense of foreboding, she rose from the deck chair, spun on her sneakers and retreated inside, firmly shutting the door behind her. Pity it couldn't be locked.

A sense of troubled anxiety took hold of Billie that night. The darkness and quiet magnified even the slightest sound so when the first daylight appeared, it was with a deep feeling of relief. She had come to the lake for some rural calm and distance but, right now, felt a rising sense of unease.

Mid-morning, as Billie lounged before the fire in the sitting room, she sat up, alert at the sound of a heavy rumbling engine growing louder. Like a four wheel drive. Another visitor. Not Noah then. He drove a rattly old ute.

Footsteps sounded on the deck outside and a face peered in at one of the windows. Her heart jumped in fright. It was one of the guys driving the utes yesterday at the plane pickup. Billie had seen him but believed he hadn't noticed her or he would have come after her at the time, not driven away. The stocky build, face full of whiskers and cap on backwards suggested a person who, at first sight, you might not be inclined to trust.

Although they had clearly locked eyes in shock at seeing each other now – or was it only on her part, Billie wondered – he moved away from the window and thumped on the door.

She rose, glancing around for something she could grab as a weapon if needed. Her toasting fork rested on the hearth but that would look a bit obvious and dramatic so she straightened, took a deep breath and stepped across the room to meet her guest. Revisiting Noah's words in her mind and prophetic caution about being a woman alone out here.

Billie deliberately stood in the open doorway blocking entry to the shack. She folded her arms and stared him down. 'Yes?'

'Morning. Shack's usually empty. What are you doing here?'

'Minding my own business and keeping to myself. You could try doing the same.'

'You're on private property.'

Where had she heard that before? 'I know. So are you. Unless you're a Lowe and, like me, have permission.'

Her confidence surprised him for a moment because he checked himself, then scowled, assessing her. 'You hiding from someone?'

'None of your business. Leave me in peace and I'll return the favour.'

'How do you know I live around here?'

Billie narrowed her gaze and gave a casual shrug, as though her insides weren't churning over and she was as calm as she pretended. 'I don't. But since the dirt road to this shack is hardly on a highway, I presume you're local. I'd appreciate you keeping your distance and not bothering me again.'

'Back at you, lady.'

Just when Billie expected him to leave, he stepped forward, closer. Too close. Even though she was taller and looked down on him slightly into his face, she was repulsed by his foul warm breath on her skin and crawled with loathing. Her anxiety kicked into overdrive and his creepy threatening attitude filled her with alarm. Hoping she didn't need to use her taekwondo skills, she adjusted her stance anyway to be ready for him if he made a move against her.

As he half turned aside, he growled, 'I'll be keeping an eye on you.'

He had barely walked off when Billie slammed the door, swiped up her phone and raced through the shack to the bathroom so she could snap a photo of the number plate through the small high window before he drove away. Standing to one side and staying hidden until it was safer, she noticed his vehicle was the same black four wheel drive from yesterday. The rego could be a fake but she knew Ewan Holt could find out if it was genuine and the owner's identity.

She hid from view until the man slid into the car and out of her vision before she moved forward, aimed her mobile, zoomed in on the rear and clicked.

Billie slid to the bathroom floor to sit a moment, gather up her composure and try to steady her thudding heart. This innocent and humble little bush shack, at the very least, was starting to feel like a place of threat, right on the back doorstep of trouble, a danger to her safety and solitude. If it wasn't drugs, it was something else illegal or she wouldn't have been paid such a threatening visit.

She groaned at the idea of telling the police her suspicions and threats. So far, she reasoned, they were simply that. Suspicions. But government televisions ads advised that if you saw something that didn't look right to call it in. Common sense told her that was the way to go.

She knew Ewan Holt from recently supporting Piper Thorne in dealing with the thieves who stole her valuable family artefact. She should drive into the local police station, speak to him and quietly express her concerns. He might be prepared to believe and investigate her fears.

Billie gave herself a good shake, managed to stand and walk back through the shack to brew another strong coffee and a snack for lunch. While the kettle boiled, her thoughts slowed to steady and more reasonable.

Maybe she should just do like her visitor suggested and stay put. It was none of her business. Was she simply being paranoid, over anxious after all that had occurred recently in her life? Should she simply ignore everything and pretend nothing was happening around her? Chill like she planned and put a brake on her imagination? Focus on her future. Where it might be. What she wanted as a single woman again. An outcome she was far from reaching.

Billie sighed. The anticipated *quiet life* she was experiencing in her hideaway on the lake sounded far more exciting. Perhaps because of its inherent risk. An element of life which had always appealed to her. Like helping Piper recently. The thrill of a challenge. Taking up a dare. Tempting trouble. Meanwhile, ignoring her purpose for coming to the shack. Today, she had been warned off but living with memories of a challenging childhood, and after recently having her heart trampled, she had long ago grown a strong obstinate streak.

After her surprise visitor earlier, it only confirmed in Billie's mind that something definitely dodgy was happening with that float plane and its regular trips to the lake. Those blokes certainly weren't angling for redfin. Not a fishing rod in sight. And they didn't hang around. Were barely at the jetty for more than ten minutes, hardly spoke to each other then disappeared to every point of the compass in a flash.

Bad enough to approach the police and be turned away in embarrassment for lack of any solid proof. It would be even worse tempting fate and their friendship to confide in Noah. He had warned her to stay up this end of the lake. As a local, if he knew of any shady activity at Willow Bend, he would report it, Billie was sure. He would never turn a blind eye against anything illegal. Noah Sutton was no coward. He had deliberately volunteered and signed up for military duty. Billie was willing to bet he wouldn't back away from a fight. He would be in the thick of it.

Bottom line, she knew she would be safe confiding in him. He may not like that she had gone off snooping again but he would listen.

Besides, he didn't need to know every detail and she could fudge the truth.

First up, she decided to head over to the Sutton farm and gauge Noah's reaction to what she had witnessed at the lake this morning and the threatening guest who had paid her a visit. At least she now had a starting point with the four wheel drive number plate. Billie needed to find out exactly what Noah knew because it was definitely more than he was letting on.

By early afternoon, hating herself for making the effort, Billie changed clothes into jeans, boots and a long flattering sweater, running a brush through her shoulder length hair and spreading a peachy gloss over her lips. She could have stayed in her lounging gear and hiked across the paddock to his place. As the crow flies, it was probably only a few kilometres but she didn't want to arrive all sweaty and messy. The SUV it was.

Noah Sutton and his older brother, Adam, had been a few classes higher than her at school but she well knew the family and where they lived.

Billie climbed into her sporty blue car for the first time in a week and returned to the main road. From memory, it was the first house and next property north.

The name on the mailbox at the roadside was a giveaway so she turned in. A short gravelled drive led to the first house, fenced off from the rest of the farmland and surrounding machinery sheds, workshops and outbuildings.

The red brick home where Bill and Margaret Sutton had lived, and where Noah and Adam would have grown up, was neat but looked deserted. All the curtains were drawn and the garden was overgrown, clearly neglected. Billie stopped and stepped out, wandering around the house and yard, calling out from time to time. There was no sight or sound of any people about nor vehicles parked anywhere near so Billie climbed back into her car and drove across a short paddock track to the second farmhouse.

On the approach, she passed small sheds, poultry freely wandering and scratching in the grass outside their fenced yard, its gate wide open. An old timber single car garage was empty, its double doors sagging as though they were never shut. Finally, she sighted Noah's ute parked outside an older original weatherboard homestead she believed probably belonged to his grandparents.

He was bending over a work bench cutting timber with a hand saw. He must have heard her arrival but kept working and only glanced over his shoulder after she pulled up and sauntered around into his line of sight.

Billie leaned back against his ute, arms folded, and waited. Peeped into the rear tray of the vehicle behind her, filled with all the usual farming stuff. Toolbox, fuel cans and what was probably useful junk. Your typical workhorse farm vehicle.

As she turned her gaze back to watch Noah work for a moment until he finished, the beautiful black and white Border Collie that had been playing further away now raced back toward them, making straight for Billie.

'Buddy,' Noah commanded quietly, straightening and adding his freshly cut length of wood to a pile nearby.

The animal sat on its haunches, looking up at Billie, head tilted to one side. He had the most intelligent eyes and she reached out to stroke him. 'Hey Buddy,' she said softly.

When she glanced up, Billie caught her breath. Noah Sutton was the whole package. Dusty jeans and boots, untucked and half unbuttoned checked flannel shirt flying open, its sleeves rolled up to the elbows. He was an impressive piece of human farm equipment. Drool worthy stuff.

He caught her fixed concentration and slowly smiled. Almost devilish. 'You're staring.'

'Just appreciating a fit man. He's lovely.' She nodded down at the dog, swinging the conversation away from personal.

'He could wreak havoc when he's bored if I let him so I keep him busy. Excellent watch dog. I bought him as a puppy from working lines. I recently invested in stud Merinos and he's already becoming a great herding dog. Plan to build up a flock. Buddy here will help keep them in line.' Noah approached and ruffled the dog's head then indicated toward the front steps leading up to the veranda. 'Come and sit.'

He perched on the second step and the dog settled at his feet. Billie followed and sat beside Noah. She watched his calloused working man's hands rub the animal's head between the ears while the dog looked up at his master with loyal eyes.

She wouldn't have thought such a physically strong man could have such a gentle touch. Only contact she remembered growing up was a hard slap from her father, Jack, and her oldest brother, Johnny, when he realised he could repeat their father's actions and get away with it.

Noah jumped right to the point. 'What did you do?'

Billie raised her eyebrows. 'Why do you assume I did anything?'

'Wondering why you're here. This a social visit then?'

Billie wavered. 'Sort of. I'd appreciate your opinion.' She pulled a face. 'Yeah. Starting to feel like Bourke Street over there. So much for my privacy.'

'Sounds like you have a problem.'

Nothing for it but to leap right into her real purpose for calling in on a neighbour. 'I was out walking yesterday and saw a float plane land on the lake.'

Noah's head snapped around and his blue eyes drilled her with attention.

'Walking helps me sort out my thoughts,' she explained, surprised by the depth of his disapproval.

'I thought I told you to stay around the shack.'

It was way more than male ego. He sounded genuinely concerned for her safety. Which only raised even more questions beyond those she already had as to why Noah thought she might be in danger. He *had* to know something she didn't. 'You don't think that's unusual?'

He hedged. 'What exactly did you see?'

Billie wasn't sure if he was simply interested or digging for information. And he hadn't answered her questions.

'A float plane land and tie up at the jetty. Just on sunrise yesterday. It seemed odd when I first heard and saw it flying low. I thought it was in trouble. Plus something didn't feel right so I watched from behind cover. Glad I did. At first there wasn't anyone else about but when the plane tied up at the jetty, utes and four wheel drives came out of nowhere. Guys jumped out and looked in an awful hurry to unload heaps of boxes. Didn't stick around for more than ten minutes before they left and the plane took off again. Pilot couldn't have been too friendly.

Didn't even see him. He stayed in the plane.'

Noah seemed to relax a little at her explanation and shrugged. 'Probably just bringing in farm supplies.'

Billie scoffed. 'By plane? Why not trucks?'

'Maybe it was difficult access where they needed to go.'

'It was only small stuff. And the way they were handling the goods meant it wasn't fragile.' Billie madly shook her head. 'Easily carried by a man and transported in any farm vehicle, even without any track across a paddock.' She frowned and stared south toward the lake sheltered and hidden by bushland in the distance. 'If you could see the smoke at the shack from here, you could even see or hear a plane.'

Noah slightly shifted his gaze, avoiding her eyes. 'Have to be honest, I didn't see anything from here.'

Billie released a deep frustrated sigh. 'Then there was a drone late yesterday. Out over the lake. Near the shack. Felt creepy.'

'Could have been anyone out to play with a techie gadget. Drones are popular these days.' Again, Noah appeared interested yet untroubled by all the events she was describing.

'Maybe,' Billie shrugged, 'but they have restrictions. That wasn't the worst of it. A dodgy guy paid me a visit this morning. Definitely not friendly and warning me off.'

'The guy might be like me and saw smoke

from the shack chimney and checked out of concern.'

'You were friendly,' Billie muttered. 'This guy was downright hostile.'

'My advice is still the same. Stay out of sight and keep to yourself. You're a woman alone. Not everyone is a good human being.'

'That's why I came here and what I've been doing. Minding my own business but all this stuff is happening around me.' Billie found herself growing irritated by Noah's casual attitude. In her mind, it was all raising loads of questions and he wasn't coming forward with any answers. 'You don't see anything unusual about a float plane that would be more at home in Alaska?'

Noah's chuckle broke the tension of differences in the air. Billie pushing her points. Noah annoyingly cool. 'Not really. May mean nothing at all.'

Billie wasn't convinced. 'It's all too much of a coincidence.'

'This farm joins the Lowe property and its mostly vacant homestead,' Noah said easily. 'He might have been a local simply casing out the nearest neighbours. Checking everything was all right by the lake.'

'What if he's a stranger? Poking around on private property asking questions?'

'Right now,' Noah offered, 'I can't explain anything to you but if it eases your mind, I'll look into it. Call in and have a chat to Ewan Holt at the station. See if he's heard anything that might tie in with what you saw.'

Billie considered that a good idea. Ewan might take more notice of another man, especially someone as highly respected as Noah Sutton in the district. All the same, accustomed to being in charge and taking control, she couldn't help suggesting, 'I could come along with you?'

Noah pulled a slow grin. 'You could but you're supposed to be having a break. I'm happy to do it. I'm in and out of town most days. Not a problem.'

'All right. Thanks. I thought about doing the same thing. Oh and I took a photo of the vehicle registration number.'

'You did?'

'Clever huh?'

'You okay about sending it to my phone?' He fished his mobile out of a pocket.

'Sure.' Billie transferred it across to him.

'Got it. I'll let you know if Ewan has any concerns or further information when he puts the number through the system and checks it out. Should at least give us a name and address. If the plates are authentic.'

'Great.' Billie's mind eased after sharing her concerns and receiving Noah's readiness to help. Maybe Ewan would find some answers and end her worries. Finally allowing herself to relax a little, she squinted out around the paddocks. 'Ever get lonely living out here on your own?'

'Don't mind it.'

'It's so quiet at the lake. Mostly,' she said dryly.

'It's called peace, Billie.' Noah gave a low chuckle. 'Soak it up. Free benefit of living in the country.'

'Yeah. All a state of mind really, right?' She grinned and sighed. 'Brings back early childhood memories of living here.'

'Good ones?'

Billie reflected and shrugged. 'A few. When I was really young. Before dad could no longer resist the drink and our family life went sour. I remember a time or two going down to Longerenong Creek at the back of Addie Kendall's parents' property on school camps. Felt like such freedom to be out of our house in town. Miles away from reality, you know?'

'Sounds like the shack.'

'True.'

Noah rose and descended the steps, turning to Billie and extending a hand. 'Up for a farm tour?' When she hesitated, he teased, 'Can't tell me you don't have time.'

'Not interrupting your work?'

'Due for a break.'

She reached out and accepted, his rough firm grip pulling her up to stand before him.

'Thanks,' she muttered, suddenly feeling

dangerously affected by that great body so close and awkwardly trying to ignore it.

He strode across to the ute and opened the passenger door. 'Jump in.' As he moved around to the other side, he whistled to Buddy who leapt into the back tray.

'Where are we going?'

'To check out the Merinos I bought recently. My flock of girls and a few bad boys. Most important members of the flock.'

'You're not going to tell me rams have the same ego as men.'

He simply grinned but didn't comment. The ute bumped along a track, through an open gate and across a grassy paddock. At the far end, Noah pulled up, left the engine running and rested his arms comfortably on the steering wheel.

'Because my property acreage has been reduced, I'm setting up a mixed farm. That's my new line of breeding ewes.' He nodded over the fence. 'What do you think?'

'They look woolly and impressive.'

'Might try some crossbreeds, too, for fat lambs. It's all trial and error at the moment until I find my feet. The local farmer who sold them to me is respected and happy to pass on his experience and knowledge.'

'Sounds like you have a challenging and planned future ahead of you.'

Billie only wished she was as certain as

Noah about her own outlook. At the moment, she was taking one day at a time and thinking of the weeks and months ahead, not years. Which included not simply her personal life but career vision as well. Did she even want to stay in accounting? She was damn good at it and thrived on its challenges but did she want to be doing it forever?

'You've turned quiet,' Noah said softly, backing up the ute and turning around.

'If I'm honest, guess I'm envious. You know what you want.'

'Took a while. No future comes with guarantees.'

As Noah drove them back between paddocks and out onto an unsealed road, Billie couldn't help but reflect and compare this man to her ex-fiancé. The man she had been about to marry! To her embarrassment, she realised in all the years she had been in a partnership with David, they never really sat down like this and talked. It was all business and social life and what was happening in each of their work places. Almost like living on the surface and never delving deeper.

Despite her initial reservations about Noah's character, Billie felt comfortable in his presence, talking, confiding. Knowing she wasn't being judged or needed to live up to certain expectations. He took her at face value as a flawed human being. And aren't we all, she thought?

'Jump out.'

Sunk deep in thought, Billie noticed they had stopped on the roadside and Noah was climbing out. Buddy leapt from the back and raced around them as they walked toward a fence. She followed. Leaning on a fence post beside Noah, a stiff winter breeze blowing back the ends of her shoulder length hair, Billie gazed out across a healthy-looking grain crop.

'Wheat or barley? They both look the same to me.'

'Barley. Wheat's in the next paddock west. Come summer I'll hire contractors for the harvest. Not invest in expensive machinery yet until I'm more established and discover if I've inherited my father and grandfather's farming skills.'

Billie secretly eyed Noah alongside. 'You're a planner with a strategy. Property and stock look healthy. Can hardly see failure in your future.'

'Thanks for the encouragement. When I returned, I wasn't sure I would stay. I left home at 18 and hardly ever came back. When I did, I never really helped my dad on the farm. After Adam was killed, walls came up for everyone and it was never the same. This time around, once I was here, I figured I might as well renovate the old house.'

Noah went quiet, frowning. 'Wasn't a

choice. The house where I grew up holds too many ghosts. I have happier memories of my grandparents' old timber homestead. Before all the tragedy.'

Billie reached out and silently laid a hand on his arm. Eventually he continued.

'But when it was time for cropping, the paddocks had been idle for two years so I decided to plant some grain. Talking to a few older farmers who knew my dad, they suggested raising livestock might be another way to go. So,' he turned to look at her, grinning, 'I'm developing a mixed property.'

'Sounds to me like you've inherited plenty of farming blood. I'm sure you'll do just fine.'

'I'm taking one season at a time. Dealing with whatever comes up. Learning on my feet.'

Billie sighed. It all sounded so idyllic and *possible*. If only her own life had a roadmap. She rubbed her arms, not against the cold winter wind but a ripple of nervous chill.

'Feeling cold?' Noah asked.

Billie shook her head, touched by his caring tone. David had been like that. Once.

Pushing her thoughts in a more positive direction, she said, 'I know I've become a city person living among skyscrapers and concrete but I love to walk and run. Especially through parklands.' She shrugged. 'Which sometimes means getting in your car for a decent drive to find one. Nature isn't at your doorstep like out here.' She spun for a 180 view. 'No buildings or people in sight. I'd forgotten the precious freedom of that.'

On the way back to the house block, Noah was obviously driving her by the scenic route, taking her further around the district, past other farms and lush green crops before they returned to the old homestead again.

Billie eyed it fondly as she climbed from the ute. It certainly was a grand place with verandas all round. But when she expressed interest in having a look around, Noah seemed reluctant to invite her inside, yet he had willingly taken her around the farm to show her his sheep and crops.

'It's dangerous in places. A few floor boards are still missing,' he remarked.

Billie didn't feel quite so excluded once she realised Noah's hesitation was out of concern for her welfare.

'I'm light on my feet. I'll be careful,' she reassured him. Cheekily deciding to take the matter into her own hands, she laughed and leapt the broad front steps, turning back to watch for his reaction. 'Coming?'

Hands on hips, shaking his head and with a tolerant grin teasing that inviting mouth, Noah followed and opened the door for her to step inside.

The old homestead's interior was gutted and rough. Noah was clearly planning a thorough genuine renovation and taking it back to its bones.

'The rooms are huge,' Billie said with admiration. 'Is that your mattress on the floor?'

He didn't look the slightest bit uncomfortable about her observation. 'Easier to live here while I work on it between farming. Saves constantly hiking between the two houses. Power and water are still connected. Besides, furniture isn't practical until I've finished the floors.'

Billie guessed having completed a decade of military service had prepared him for basic living conditions. 'It has huge potential.' She peered into each of many rooms, some with fireplaces.

'Careful,' he murmured, catching her arm as they moved into the main living and kitchen areas where she noticed the timber floor boards missing as he had warned.

'Thanks. I see them.'

Still reeling from a relationship gone bad, Billie was shocked that Noah's touches and concern could affect her so deeply in the most warmly disturbing way. *Careful,* she told herself, *attentions fade.*

Following her gaze over the stripped-back kitchen, sporting only an old black wood stove, he said, 'It's been unoccupied for years and seen better days but as I find the time I'm working at it. Still remember my grandmother cooking on that beast. I'll replace it with a modern electric country cooker.'

'Sounds like you intend living here.'

Noah shrugged. 'Hadn't thought that far ahead.'

'Seems a shame when you put all your love and sweat into it.'

'Didn't like to see such a grand old place getting worse. Just trying to save it, I guess. In honour of my grandparents. Keep some family heritage.'

Billie respected and envied his strong connection to family and this land. A farm seeing its next generation take over the reins. Maybe the pull had been stronger than his instincts and drawn him back against his will.

'What about your parents' house next door?' In the country, *next door* could mean kilometres away.

'It needs updating, too. Cosmetic stuff really. I'm still going through stuff in cupboards and sheds on the place.'

Billie had to wonder if Noah's old homestead renovation was avoiding the reality of returning home alone to the farm and having to deal with facing the task of sifting through a lifetime of family memories, which he had already admitted was proving difficult. Noah Sutton wasn't out of the woods yet either. In his case, confronting the hard truth of being the sole survivor after his brother, Adam, died in his prime. The joint deaths of possibly lonely grieving parents more recently who may never have recovered from the loss of their older son would challenge even the strongest person. Not helped by his long absences on service overseas and rare visits back to the Wimmera. On purpose, Billie speculated?

'I should let you get on. Thanks for your hospitality. I've enjoyed it. Neighbour,' she added with a grin.

'For now,' he said softly.

Billie felt a nudge of regret hearing Noah voice the reality of her temporary stay.

Back outside again as they stood and faced each other before Billie left, Noah reached out and gently placed a hand on her shoulder. The gesture and its intended reassurance caught her off guard. She felt her emotions for him stir again.

'Be careful,' he said softly.

She was filled with guilt for feeling so protected by this man, not to mention incredibly attracted. 'I told you not to worry about me,' she said lightly to ease the mood.

'I can't help it.' He paused. 'You're-'

'Not helpless.'

This close, she wondered if he felt the same pull of attraction. The teasing warmth in his voice hinted at a certain amount of flirty awareness. But was the suggestion of tenderness in those blue eyes her imagination? Before she made a move she might regret, Billie backed away, breaking contact.

She jumped in before he had a chance to say something nice that would really send her sensations haywire.

With a smile and a wave, she drove away, aware she had definitely learnt more about Noah Sutton. Today had been revealing and engaging. And, damn it, she really liked what she saw. But was it wise?

She had a life to reset and needed all her focus on that. Time to take her swinging emotions in hand and deal with her past life before she embarked on a new one.

Chapter 4

Two nights later, as Billie went to draw down the window blinds just on dark, she noticed lights flashing in the distance. Looked like it was out in the middle of the lake, possibly in bushland at Willow Bend.

Even as she wondered about the wisdom of pursuing the idea that had popped into her mind, she made a snap decision. Throwing on a waterproof coat and beanie, mobile tucked safely into a zipped pocket and grabbing a torch, she went to investigate.

It would take longer to jog around the lake at night but the small row boat was still floating next to the deck. She figured it must be watertight without leaks or it would have sunk by now so Billie scrambled in, grabbed the oars, untied the rope and tossed it between her legs then started to row. Hard.

Halfway to Willow Bend, rowing so strongly and with such purpose her arms ached, Billie realised that although she had been indoors, she hadn't heard a plane tonight and it was already dark. Would an aircraft land at this late time of day? Maybe the lights were somehow connected to the plane activity.

All this effort and assumption could be for nothing. Still, she pushed on. She had to find out who or what was out there. Not having heard anything further from Noah since his promise to have a chat to Ewan Holt, she needed to check out if the situation was suspicious but she had no idea or plan what she could do about it.

As she drew close, fearing her splashing oars might be heard, Billie stopped rowing and let the boat glide into the reeds. Loud voices and laughing, both male and female, echoed from the nearby bushland. In her curiosity, her big mistake was pushing through the thick and high waterside grasses. Waterbirds, having sought shelter for sleep and believing themselves safe from predators, grew unsettled. Disturbed, they woke with noisy quacking and flapping.

Billie froze and grew still.

A male voice asked, 'Did you hear something?'

'Just birds, dude.'

'They're probably having sex, mate. Leave them alone.'

Laughter erupted as the group's conversation returned to a murmur again. She was about to relax when Billie heard trampling through the undergrowth and a torch was flashed about. She couldn't see anyone which she hoped meant they couldn't see her, and held her breath.

As a precaution and panicking at the possibility of being discovered in such an embarrassing situation, Billie decided she needed to hide. Slowly and quietly easing herself from the boat, she slid into the water and gasped. It was freezing. She looped the rope among the tall reed stalks and stayed still, hoping the lack of movement would resettle the birds.

Eventually, she heard the torch click off and the person's footsteps fade. Sounded like a bunch of local young people, all probably simply drinking, smoking and laughing around a campfire, just out for a night together.

After Billie realised the lights certainly hadn't come from who she suspected and this whole useless experience was a crazy and unnecessary waste of time and effort, she grew mad at herself for pointlessly getting cold and wet. Talk about an alarmist. Not usually her style or reaction of being in control. She was allowing her mind to play games over her normal logic.

With great effort she stayed in the water, swimming and pulling the boat by the rope behind her until she reached shallower water closer to the lake's edge. Although sodden and heavy, she somehow managed to haul herself back into the boat, resting for a moment before taking up the oars again and slowly rowing her way back to the shack.

It seemed to take forever and, despite her usually high level of fitness, she felt drained.

Before she reached the deck, a dark figure rose in shadow from the chair by the door. Reeling in fright, thinking it was the guy come to pay another threatening visit, or worse, she sucked in deep breaths to calm her pounding heart.

Until she recognised who it was. While Billie sagged with relief, she also knew her evening was not about to improve.

'Taking a midnight swim?' Noah stood hands on hips above her.

'Not voluntarily.' Billie tied the boat to the corner post and, shivering, wearily stepped out, stomping on the deck to shake off as much water as possible.

'Did you fall out?'

'No!'

'Why are you out at night? Where on earth have you been?'

'Really. So many questions. I'll tell you when I'm warm and dry.' She moved past him. As she walked inside and crossed the living room, Billie tossed over her shoulder, 'Make yourself useful and stoke that fire while I change.'

Her sharpness arose from a personal sense of annoyance. Why did Noah Sutton have to be here tonight of all nights catching her out in an embarrassing moment? She sighed. Somehow she didn't feel she would ever measure up or manage to appear composed and together around him.

Billie peeled off her soggy clothes and dropped them on the bathroom floor. She didn't want to waste water with even the recommended five minute shower so just briskly towelled herself down and dragged on a tracksuit and thick socks.

When she reappeared, Noah had the fire roaring again. Standing to one side, his arm on the mantel, he growled, 'Damn it, woman. I told you to stick around the shack.' When she didn't respond, he added, 'You don't take advice well.'

'So I've been told.' She crossed to the fire and knelt before its soothing flames, threading her fingers through her damp hair ends to loosen and dry.

'Nice diversion,' Noah chuckled. Deep and throaty and lovely. 'Why do I get the feeling you never quite tell me everything?'

After their first meeting, Billie had been inclined to have similar reservations about him. 'Have you seen Ewan Holt?' He nodded. 'Any news?'

'He's looking into it.'

'Whatever that means.'

'So, what happened?'

'I noticed lights on Willow Bend,' she admitted softly, her back turned toward him. 'I thought it might be something suspicious and went to check it out.'

'Of course you would. Why did you end up in the water?'

'For safety.'

Noah pushed out a burst of exasperation. 'You're a smart woman, Billie. I don't get that you would go out on your own at night like this.'

'In hindsight, I have absolutely no idea either.'

'Glad you thought it through,' he drawled. 'And what did you find that needed investigation at midnight?'

'It's not midnight!' He raised his eyebrows, waiting for an answer. 'Nothing but a bunch of kids around a campfire,' she mumbled, embarrassed.

Despite misreading the situation and her soggy ending, it *had* been a tiny adventure out there. Besides, she had always been active and it grew a bit tiresome sitting around relaxing all day. The reason she rarely took holidays. So she didn't take Noah's displeasure too deeply to heart, pretty much ignored it, although she didn't doubt it was given out of concern. Which he was totally not hiding beneath a mountain of male attitude.

To make up for her grumpy reaction to his arrival, Billie decided she should be hospitable and rose from the fire, moving into the kitchenette to boil the kettle.

Noah ambled across the room and leaned against the counter beside her, arms crossed, disturbingly close. 'I know you haven't asked but can I give you my opinion for free?'

'Do I have a choice?' She set out mugs and coffee.

'Always.'

'Can I stop you?'

'Probably not. If I have you pegged right, you're not short of confidence but not stupid. So what you did tonight,' his voice had softened and he paused, 'was reckless, seems kind of out of character and erratic. Upshot of whatever's just happened in your life?'

Billie was jolted by his observation. Of course she was unsettled. Her bum fiancé who she had been prepared to accept as her partner for life, had just decided she was dispensable. Had it clouded her thinking, like, tonight? An excuse for avoiding working out her future. She couldn't say but Noah's quiet perception and courage to voice it, caught her off guard. The guy's nature was challenging and more upfront than she felt comfortable with right now.

'I saw it while I was in service,' he went on, 'out in the field overseas and afterwards when we returned from missions. It takes time to work through personal emotions like pain and distress.'

Billie cringed, feeling sick in the stomach at Noah's accuracy. She was honest and intelligent enough to know he was right. Except in her case he didn't know the details but was perceptive enough to notice likely symptoms. So she'd probably be helping herself if she confronted and faced her unfortunate truth. Focusing on the plane and its cargo drop, probably lifting that situation out of all proportion to its importance when she should have left such matters to the law, had been an avoidance tactic not worthy of her intelligence.

She came out here to get away from her heartbreak, discovered she couldn't escape it. Now this guy was dragging it out into the open. She had to wonder if a decade of working in war and conflict zones made Noah so wise or if his own strength and resilience could not only deal with it, but help others try to achieve the same.

His shoulders lifted into a shrug, brushing gently against her. 'Wanna talk, I'm always here.'

When the kettle sang, she asked, 'Tea or coffee?' half turning toward him and giving herself time to recover some sense of composure.

'Surprise me.'

He wasn't being polite, trying to make the decision easier or please her. She gained the impression this man genuinely did not sweat the small stuff. Having survived hostilities and disasters overseas, she assumed it brought into focus what was really base level important to a person in life.

If her few days here on the lake already were any indicator, she was beginning to grasp it was probably the simple pleasures. Maybe her childhood had been more of an advantage than she appreciated at the time, despite the underlying aggression.

'How do *you* deal with the effects of trauma?' Billie asked softly.

'I work with it. Every single day. And I'm grateful for my dog's mateship. Unconditional loyalty there.' He paused, frowning. 'Plus I lost my brother when I was still young so I guess my education into tragedy and hard knocks started early. But first you gotta admit the bad memories before you can deal. Know what I'm saying?'

Billie nodded. 'Sure.'

Hiding her feelings and now being tactfully reminded she must eventually face them, made Billie feel like she was about to crack. What spirit out there, she wondered, had brought this man into her world, knowing she could do with a sensitive friend who understood? It was a bigger question than she could answer.

She made two mugs of coffee with sugar, handed one to Noah and grabbed an opened packet of bought biscuits. They were both drawn back toward the roaring fire and sat opposite.

Billie set the biscuits on the mat between them, took a deep breath and blurted out, 'Basically my fiancé dumped me.'

Scary admission but it was out. And it felt good. She hadn't actually voiced to anyone about having her heart broken and how deeply it cut. She waited a moment, braved a glance at Noah for any reaction and watched as his brow furrowed.

He leant forward, resting his arms on his knees, mug cradled in his hands. 'I'm sorry.'

The gentle frank sentiment almost crumbled her composure. Before she changed her mind, Billie launched into the painful details.

'His name is David. A lovely conservative, traditional name, right? We met in my first year at university. He was five years older and finishing law. Pretty much instant chemistry. I was smitten. He was the exact opposite of any man I had ever met until then. Polished. A gentleman. Kind. Classically handsome. Had everything going for him really.

'He used to look at me with such love and devotion. As though I was the most precious thing in the world to him. His gazes and perception were so intense I almost saw myself through his eyes. He would so gently place his hand on my back and walk beside me, ushering me into a room. I felt so special. Wanted. A part of him. Wasn't long before we were living together and I eventually found myself with a diamond sparkling on my finger, tossing around wedding dates. It wasn't a whirlwind but it was…heady. I thought I was safe.'

Her voice cracked. When she took a sip of coffee for composure, she discovered her hands were shaking.

'Incredibly, *that* was when he changed. After our engagement. Over time, the distance grew. Slid away in such small pieces and barely noticeable. At first, he was just that second too late with a gesture or small show of attention when he was usually so gracious to me. I noticed, but thought he was distracted or busier than usual. But gradually he did it less until eventually the tiny gems of consideration stopped altogether. I tried harder to be what I thought he wanted me to be. More of this or less of that.'

'Unlike you,' Noah drawled with a grin.

'Yeah, I know, right? I've kind of dug in my heels here, haven't I? Been obstinate out of rebellion. To hide the ache.'

Tears pooled in her eyes. She sniffed, breathed deeply to steady her upheaval then went on.

'Despite the signs, I refused to believe what was happening with David. What we had. It died. At least on his part. But it was also clear to me that we didn't have *anything* anymore. I'm a woman of the world. I know relationships aren't necessarily forever. I'd seen friends who I thought were solid couples dissolving all around me. Personal partnerships in all their forms are tricky little suckers. You just never know.' Billie heaved a shaky sigh of regret. 'You just never.'

She grew silent, staring into the flames, knowing the reason for her wrecked future was still raw and sharp. 'Turns out all the while my engagement was dissolving, David and my best friend, Julia, had already plunged into a steamy liaison. Almost a year later when he stood in front of me that night and told me the truth, I was stunned. He fell all over himself with apologies saying *It just happened.* Under my nose? With my best friend? Former best friend,' Billie muttered. 'I mean, how blind could I have been?'

Billie finished her coffee and settled back further into the sofa. 'After I rented a new apartment, I soon discovered it was a huge mistake. I had to get away somewhere for a while. When I dumped my misery on Sasha, she offered me the shack so I grabbed it. Anywhere near my home town sounded good to me. Comforting.

'I didn't immediately head up here to the Wimmera. I figured on giving myself about two weeks. My time was my own so instead of heading north I turned west and drove along the Great Ocean Road. Eventually, I turned inland again heading up to Hamilton. Somehow the road signs pointing toward the Grampians mountains caught my fancy so I found myself taking a detour and driving into Dunkeld in the southern foothills.

'Talk about fate.' Billie related the whole series of episodes and encounters with Piper Thorne. 'You would know her.'

Noah nodded. 'Their family is prominent in the local indigenous community.'

'We were all at school together. Sasha Lowe, Addie Kendall, Piper and me. After Piper's grandmother died, she set out to search for an old artistic bark painting relic that had been stolen from her family some years ago. She found it and got it back. She saw me in Dunkeld and we chatted for a moment. I was feeling rubbish, so I'm afraid I wasn't too polite. The mountain air and Piper's enthusiasm for the village got to me, I guess, because next thing I knew I had booked a few nights at a B&B.

'Talk about a sudden change of pace. Driving along the coast I was still wired from breaking with David. That my best friend would be so disloyal, chat excitedly with me over lunch and a glass of wine making wedding plans, and lie for almost a year about the fact that she linked up with my fiancé before I finally learnt the truth.

'By the time I made Dunkeld, my usual fast pace of life had slowed because I was back in familiar country again. I went for walks and drives, stopped for coffee or lunch in the café. Winding back dragged my mind to calmer thoughts. Incredibly, the day I planned to leave, Piper Thorne caught my eye across the street in town again. She was frantic. That was when she told me her friend Ben had helped her retrieve the lost family artefact and that they were panicking they would probably be followed.

'I tell you, when Piper told me the story about being deceived, it hit home. I was happy to help. They asked me to take the artwork and meet up with them again at the Coach Roadhouse out on the highway. I did that and Piper eventually appeared but not Ben. She grew worried. Naturally. She phoned her family and they all arrived to help so next thing I know we're heading off into the bush at Roses Gap tracking Ben on Piper's phone.'

Billie smiled at the memory, shaking her head. 'We had this crazy idea that a bunch of amateurs could take down a group of thieves. But, somehow, we did. I have to say,' she admitted proudly, 'I used some great taekwondo moves on my designated target. Then Piper's whole mob emerges from the scrub, like, maybe twenty people. And behind them, a line of police.

'The uniforms snapped handcuffs on the thieves, everyone hugged and cried, and you could just feel the relief and deep meaning that passed among Piper's whole big family.' Billie turned reflective and her voice softened. 'Made me wish among my own parents and siblings that we had all known a better experience. And then recently, of course, I wonder if that tough life didn't affect the way I lived in the city. It was all about success and possessions. Those few quiet days in Dunkeld opened my eyes to how little we really need each day without all the trappings.'

'Well, if it's any help,' Noah offered, 'speaking from my own experience, you don't start again. You just pick up the pieces and move on. Push forward with your life.'

'I guess I'll realise that one day and how to do it.' She glanced across at him, the firelight burnishing his sandy hair even more golden. 'Enough about me. What's your story?'

Noah pulled a wry smile but, without hesitation, plunged in. 'If it didn't hurt so much at the time, I might say that David was lucky. He only lost a ring. My ex-wife, Michelle, went after half the farm.'

Billie's response was barely a whisper. 'Ouch.'

'After my folks died, I only had five days compassionate leave. She told me then. It was a double hit but, truth is, I didn't care. I suspected our marriage was over before that. I know it was tough being a military wife. She was a city woman living away from her family out here in the country with my parents. I wasn't surprised.

'Each time I came home, it wasn't long before I was sent off on another tour of duty. It was my career. After your pilot training, you commit to ten years of active service. I warned her when we met but-' he shrugged. 'I was entitled to two weeks leave after six months. I came home but, unless both partners are determined and resilient, any relationship can lose momentum. So next time I came home, I was busy with lawyers and property agents to sell off enough land to pay her out. At least my retirement benefit on a Captain's salary helped.'

'My. *Captain* Sutton,' Billie teased, smiling.

Noah set down his empty mug on the floor and, hands clasped, stared into the orange glow of coals and lazy flames. 'Michelle did leave me something. An adorably mischievous five year old named Rosie who starts school next year. She's a little blondie like both of us.'

Billie's surprise at the announcement, and warmth in Noah's voice as he spoke about his daughter, caught her off guard. She certainly hadn't been expecting anything like that in his life. He seemed independent, even a little detached. Hiding behind personal armour against being hurt and trusting again. She understood. Had suffered, too. Loved, not so much with regret but the hindsight of learning to toughen up and grow, even from a nasty experience.

'So, Rosie lives with her mother?'

He nodded. 'Now I'm back on the farm, I see her in the kindergarten holidays and then for a week or so in the summer. My dog, Buddy, is devoted to her like you wouldn't believe. He's her watchdog and companion. When she visits, she helps me renovate the old homestead by brightening my day. I'll be seeing her soon, actually.' His eyes lit up and his expression softened. 'Her mother and the new man in her life will be away for a few weeks so Rosie wanted to stay with me. She does have grandparents in the city but apparently she asked to come to the farm. Might make a cowgirl out of her yet.'

'Sounds like she loves being in the country. Growing up out here gives you the gift of living right amongst nature. Since being back even for a short time, I acknowledge that even my own childhood, although mostly unhappy, had a few rare sweet moments to cherish. When I was away from family. They were more valuable than I realised at the time.'

Noah stretched and rose from his seat by the fire, taking up both the coffee mugs and taking them to the sink. Turning back to her, he said, 'Thanks for sharing. It's never easy. It's a gift to be allowed into another person's life. '

'Yours, too. We never really know a person simply on face value, do we?'

'Sometimes it's hard to open up. It's all about taking that first step. Speaking of steps, it's getting late. I should make tracks and let you turn in.'

They both hesitated by the door in an awkward moment of awareness. To ease his departure, Billie opened it and a chill night breeze rushed in from across the deck. Noah sank his hands into his pockets and strolled outside. For a crazy second, Billie felt the urge to grab him for a hug. Of gratitude, for being such a damn nice man. Easy company and a perceptive listener. So unlike the David's of this world.

'See you round.'

'Goodnight,' she murmured. After a few strides, he hesitated and half-turned. Billie shook her head and warned with a smile, 'Don't even. I'll try to do better.'

'Promise?'

She shrugged. 'We can hope.'

He chuckled and moved off into the dark toward his ute.

Chapter 5

When Billie's phone rang early the next morning, still filled with warm feelings from Noah's visit the day before, the thought flashed into her head that she wouldn't mind hearing his voice again.

'Billie, its Holly Duncan.'

'Oh, Holly. Great to hear from you.' She hoped her disappointment wasn't obvious.

'Ah, I know you said to come visit while you're at the shack. I have a day off today and I know its late notice but I wondered if I could come out?'

The note of agitation in Holly's voice raised an alarm and made Billie shelve her own trivial letdown. 'Sure. What time did you have in mind?'

'I can be there within the hour.'

'Fine. See you then.'

So when Billie heard crunching tyres roll along the driveway less than thirty minutes later, she was surprised and went out to greet her.

As Holly emerged from a sporty red two-door, her hunched shoulders and frown hinted at an inner tension Billie had sensed on the phone. Wearing comfy black stretch jeans and a black top, her guest nervously draped a bag over her shoulder and pulled a knee-length cream knit jacket around herself. The soft colour beautifully complimented the rusty hair waving around her face and drifting below her shoulders.

As Billie recalled, at the roadhouse Holly usually tied back that mane of hair, caught into a ponytail with a scarf. The woman was gorgeous and tall but Billie doubted she was aware of it.

Chattering too quickly, Holly said, 'Sorry. I know I'm early. Didn't really have anything else to do.' She waved an arm, trying for half a grin. 'I hope you don't mind. I'm not interrupting you in the middle of something?'

Judging by the haunted look clouding eyes the colour of gum leaves, the other woman lacked self-confidence and was clearly vulnerable. Emotions she hid behind her smiling waitress façade at the roadhouse. Even after all these years, her missing mother clearly weighed heavily on her mind every single day. What a burden that must be, the endless strain probably feeling much longer. Billie's heart went out to her. Time for some reassurance and support.

She stepped forward, smiling, and drew Holly into a quick hug. 'It's perfectly fine. It's lovely to have your company. I'm so pleased you took me up on my invitation. Come in.'

Holly's eyes lit up the moment she stepped inside. 'This is lovely.'

'It's pretty basic.'

'I love rustic.' She turned back and sighed over the water views stretching out behind them. 'Must be peaceful.'

When planes and drones weren't buzzing around and people driving in, Billie thought wryly. Then stopped herself. Who was she kidding? After city living for years, it surprised her that she was loving being back in the country. It was good to know she had a protective neighbour. And, she considered Holly warmly, she might be able to forge a new friendship here or, at the least, extend some genuine country hospitality and company to a woman who clearly needed it.

'It's probably too early for wine but I have a crisp rosé chilling in my bar fridge for lunch. Just salad and some leftover chicken. Tea or coffee?'

'Tea. I make and drink too much coffee when I'm at work,' she joked.

Billie was relieved to see her visitor begin to relax a little, backing up to the open fire as one was inclined to do.

'I guess the roadhouse is always so busy. How often do you manage to grab a day off?'

'I'm on duty pretty much seven days.' She shrugged. 'I don't have much else to do and Sid and Gracie appreciate it. I like keeping busy.'

Billie wondered if Holly *needed* to keep busy.

'To be honest, I get these-' Holly rubbed her arms and paused, 'episodes from time to time. Like visions or nightmares. I don't know what to call them exactly. Doctors don't really know what triggers them off. They just put it down to my sub-conscious working overtime and prescribe sedatives, so I've learnt to accept and deal with them.'

'You did seem unsettled when you arrived. Is that what happened last night?'

Holly nodded. 'I can have a great day and go to my cabin assuming I'll sleep well. I get to sleep but when I have a horrible dream, I wake up with a jolt. My mind and heart races. After that I'm too afraid to try and sleep again. It hits me when I least expect it.

'Sid and Gracie are really understanding. They know if I've had a rough night. They just tell me to scoot and I disappear for the day. Usually helps if I do something quiet like go for a walk or a long drive. Coming here settled me a bit.'

Billie hated to think about Holly's state of mind before she left the roadhouse. Her nerves still seemed rattled. Must take her a while to recover from each traumatic experience.

She waved an arm toward the wide windows and lake view. 'We have a whole lot of nature out there. Peaceful as you could want it in the bush except for birdlife on the water. We could take a stroll.'

Holly nodded keenly so, fuelled by warm drinks later, Billie laced up her sneakers and they set off along the bush tracks in the direction of Willow Bend. They walked in silence for a while. She decided not to push conversation and just allow the young woman to *be*.

Halfway around Billie asked, 'You okay?'

'I'll be fine. I've never really had a close friend since I moved to work at the roadhouse. Sid and Gracie are awesome. They mother me, you know, up to a point but I don't have much company except for the younger girls I work with part time. I've gotten to know some locals and regulars over the years but they're all usually just passing through. You know Addie Kendall?'

Billie nodded. 'Sure. We were at school together.'

'Did you hear about the body they found in that old Banyandah homestead on the neighbouring property to Addie's parent's farm? When I first heard about that it was scary.'

Billie grasped Holly would have logically wondered if it was her missing mother and her heart wrenched at the other woman's ongoing mental anguish. Her own problems suddenly seemed so small.

'Yes, my sister Meredith mentioned.'

Billie realised she always heard local hometown news from her youngest sibling who was more in touch with events and happenings.

And who also, despite a demanding career and schedule, made time to regularly visit their mother.

Hearing how deeply Holly was affected by her own missing mother, Billie felt neglectful of the woman who endured their own tough family situation to raise her children. She made a decision then and there to definitely go visit Heather. Soon. The thought of an encounter with her surly father always a deterrent. She needed to push past that fear. If busy Meredith could do it, Billie certainly could. Time to stop making excuses.

'Addie Kendall always has a smile and a chat when she comes through the roadhouse,' Holly went on, 'but I guess I'd have to say that she's still a casual acquaintance really. Because I'm not local born and raised, and only lived in the area for five years, I don't have a background with anyone much.

'When Piper Thorne needed help recently, I feel I got to know her a little better. But even locals are simply on their way to or from somewhere else. I think Piper will keep in touch. She introduced *us*,' Holly flashed a smile, 'so even though she's travelling around in that motorhome with Ben, when she returns I'm hoping she'll call in.'

They had almost reached the jetty when Billie heard a plane. Surely not! And highly unusual, totally out of the usual routine. It usually flew in early morning about sunrise or sunset. Not approaching midday. Her heart jolted as to why the change of schedule.

On the one hand, fed up with cheats and liars, her obstinate streak was bursting to dig in her heels, go and show herself, watch the plane come in and see what happened, suspecting the cargo being unloaded last time was probably illegal. She had already been warned off, well aware now that this whole situation and operation was potentially treacherous.

Yet on the other hand, knowing this, Billie didn't want to place Holly in danger so she needed to tell her the truth, what she had already seen and reported to Noah. Their best action and Billie's instinct at the moment was to turn and run. If either of them revealed themselves or headed out into the open, she just knew there would be consequences. Which weren't looking too healthy.

Even as Billie considered their options, Holly's gaze had turned skyward. 'I can see a plane through the trees. It's low over the water. I hope it isn't going to crash.' Even as she spoke, Holly picked up pace and moved toward the jetty and open ground.

Billie panicked. 'No!' she grabbed Holly's arm to slow her down.

'What's the matter?' Holly was frowning, naturally confused.

'I've seen this plane land before.'

'On water?'

'It's a float plane.'

'Really?' she beamed and began pulling away. 'I've never seen one. Let's go watch.'

This was the first time Holly had really smiled all day. Billie felt mean to rob her of this small moment of joy. 'Stop. It's dangerous.'

Holly frowned. 'I think it sounds kind of exciting.'

'No. I mean dangerous. Like, life threatening dangerous.' Billie had lowered her voice.

'Why are you whispering? We're alone.'

'Not for long.'

'How do you know that?'

'Because once the plane comes in and ties up at the jetty, we'll have company.'

'Who?'

'A heap of blokes and vehicles.'

'Doing what?'

'Unloading stuff from the plane.'

'Why is that dangerous?'

'Because they do it fast, like it's a secret. I've told my neighbour about it. He was going to report it to the police, see whether it's worth investigating.'

As they spoke and hid behind the undergrowth at the lake's edge, the plane had landed, its engine noise growing closer as it approached the jetty, then it shut off and the pilot steered it in. With only a patchy view through the branches of weeping willows trailing down to the water, Billie pulled out her mobile from a pocket, zoomed in and started taking photos. This time, if she and Holly escaped, she would forget Noah and take them straight to Ewan Holt at the police station.

As before, the moment the plane stopped, vehicles appeared from tracks through the bush. The same utes and black four wheel drive. Billie recognised the threatening man who had paid her a visit at the shack among the other same guys who all peeled out of their wheels and got to work, moving back and forth fast between them and the plane, close to where the women stayed hidden. Seeing it for the first time, Holly gaped at the rush of activity.

Obviously disappointed at missing the full float plane view and experience, perhaps forgetting Billie's warning in the excitement, Holly rose higher for a clearer look.

Billie yanked her down again. 'What the hell are you doing!' she hissed.

'Trying to get a better view of the handsome pilot.'

Billie had been focused on the men unloading their haul of boxes again, see if maybe she recognised anyone, so now she turned her attention in the opposite direction. Last time the pilot had stayed in the plane. This time he stood in full view on the jetty. The moment her gaze landed on him, she gasped in shock and disbelief.

No!

As she almost collapsed, stunned and speechless, beside her Holly scrunched up her nose. 'You know I think that guy comes through the roadhouse sometimes. Has a little girl with him. Lots of blonde curls.'

Is that why he had sounded so casual when she told him about the plane landing on the lake and her suspicions? What possible reason could he have for being involved?

Come to think of it, Billie hadn't seen Noah around for a few days, since he promised to follow up her misgivings about this very activity. But so far had done nothing. Was this why? Was he part of it?

When Billie didn't respond, Holly asked, 'Do you recognise him? Is he a local?'

'Yeah.' Billie found her voice. 'He's the neighbour I mentioned.'

'Oh.'

'He was in the Air Force. Back on the family farm now.'

Holly's mouth curled. 'That is so sick. A member of the armed forces breaking the law.'

Billie stung to hear such derision for a man who in her experience had done nothing but ooze charisma and good old fashioned courtesy and country hospitality. 'He's retired.'

'Makes no difference.'

Billie tensed in fear. 'Please don't say anything about this to anyone, okay? Until I know more.'

Holly's eyes widened. 'You can't want to protect the guy?'

'I'm not. But I also don't know exactly what this operation is out here. Please, Holly. Promise?'

Billie panicked when she hesitated for too long. 'Sure,' Holly said reluctantly, muttering, 'but I'd be phoning the police.'

At first, Billie couldn't understand Holly's fierce impatience to report a potential offender. Until she considered what had happened in the woman's past. It made sense that she would want lawbreakers to be held accountable. Because of her mother. The outcome, if it was ever known, wasn't looking optimistic. Holly would need closure and, right now, she didn't have that yet. If ever.

Privately, Billie grew ill in the stomach. Why would Noah be part of this sneaky network? Suddenly, she felt keen to leave.

'The guys are going,' Holly whispered as vehicle engines fired up again and wasted no time in disappearing.

Almost at the same time, Noah released the tie down and climbed back into the plane. Checking the cars were out of sight, Billie stood up and, filled with rebellion and disappointment, deliberately walked out into the open and onto the jetty. As she sauntered its length, the plane engine kicked into life and taxied further out onto the lake before revving up and gathering speed over the water. She heard Holly's footsteps behind her.

'Cool huh?'

Billie mumbled, defiantly hoping Noah noticed and recognised her, a pit of confused sadness she couldn't explain lying heavily in her stomach as the plane lifted off and gradually grew smaller.

The return walk to the shack was made in virtual silence. Holly must have sensed her reflective mood with little conversation exchanged between them.

'That whole plane delivery thing did feel kind of strange. Definitely not normal,' Holly agreed as they lingered over lunch, appearing brighter than when she first arrived.

'Glad you agree. I was beginning to think it was all happening in my imagination.'

'I still think you should go to the police,' Holly said honestly.

Something Billie could never do. Did that make her a bad person for witnessing a possible crime and not reporting it? What about Noah then? He had totally lied to her face, pretending he knew nothing. Warning her to stay away, not for concern but because he was involved. She stung over his betrayal. A local man so respected around here. Whom she had so freely trusted. The man she had grown to know and the man flying that plane couldn't possibly be the same person.

Weary and disheartened, Billie tried to put on a cheerful front for her guest but seeing Noah on that jetty had shot her concentration to pieces.

Being a rare and mild winter's day, Billie was pleased Holly grew relaxed enough to be lulled by the warmth of some afternoon sunshine. Not to mention a few glasses of wine. Enough to doze off in a chair out on the deck. Grateful to be left to her own tangled thoughts for a while.

Later, they shared another mug of coffee and Billie cranked up the fire for the evening. As the sun sank behind the bushland, casting shadows out over the water, she noticed Holly's initial edginess return.

'I should leave. It's getting late.'

'You won't stay for dinner? We could go into town for a pub meal or Chinese?' At Holly's hesitation, Billie teased, 'It wouldn't be on account of a certain handsome truck driver due to stop by?'

'No.' Holly blushed endearingly pink. 'I just like to get home by dark. To be honest, I find I really don't like driving at night.' She stumbled over the words, adding in a small voice, 'My mother went missing at night.'

'Oh.' Billie felt compelled to reach out and give her a warm hug. 'You be okay?'

'Yeah. I should be home in twenty minutes.'

Billie was interested to hear Holly call the

roadhouse *home*. You would think since it was the area where her mother disappeared, it would hold bad memories. But she had chosen to return to the district and had lived there for five years. Always hoping.

Chapter 6

Holly's little red car was barely out of sight when Billie grabbed her phone with its damning photographic proof, jumped into her SUV and sped to Noah's farm.

Fuelled by the deepest hurt and disbelief, she almost missed the turn off into the Sutton gate. Being late winter with the sun setting early, she flicked on her headlights. A quick circle around the first brick home, cloaked in the gloom of fading light, told her, as expected, if Noah was around he would be at the original homestead.

As she approached it driving across the paddock, her hopes dropped. There was no sign of Noah's ute and the grand old house loomed in the dusk without any lights or sign of life. Billie didn't bother to get out and walk. The deserted building bathed in shadow of dusk and unlit told the story.

She quickly wound down her window and flashed on her mobile torch but there were no sounds, no movement or barking from Buddy. So it didn't look like Noah's companion was here either.

Where had he gone after his plane flight this morning? Billie frowned in disappointment, her annoyance dropping. Just as well. Her quick temper was notorious for getting her into trouble when she should have taken a few deep breaths, giving herself time to settle.

She would approach Noah first thing in the morning when she was in a calmer frame of mind. But would still be equally distressed, she knew, with her mind racing and her body churning as she slowly turned the vehicle and drove from the property.

No surprise then that she didn't sleep well all night.

Next morning, Billie woke feeling drained and heavy from lack of sleep and the weight of what she was about to do. Noah Sutton was the second man to deceive her in months. Some track record. She sure could pick them.

She forced down a light breakfast and strong mug of coffee then braced herself and made the return trip to the neighbouring farm again. Her stomach rolled and her heart pounded at the sight of Noah's white ute. Buddy was trotting about but no sign of his master.

Billie sat in her vehicle for a moment to pull herself together, closed her eyes, took deep breaths then climbed the steps to the veranda. The front door was ajar so she didn't knock but pushed it wider. Buddy trotted up to greet her then disappeared inside.

'Anyone home?'

She heard movement from further back in the house, figured maybe Noah was in the kitchen. He appeared at the far end of the long wide hallway, unshaven, barefoot, dressed in his checked work shirt and jeans. A hand reached down to ruffle Buddy's head but his gaze settled on Billie.

'Morning.'

The dull sound of his usually brighter warm voice suggested he'd had a hard or long night, or both, and the distance between them cracked with strain from the early hour and what Billie thought of as his unusual mood. Maybe this was normal for him.

Had he seen her on the jetty as he flew away yesterday?

'I know it's early. Can I have a word?'

'Is it urgent?'

Odd response and question. Especially coming from Noah. So blunt and unfriendly. 'I believe so.'

His brow dipped into a frown and he took a few steps forward. 'There's an old sofa in the front room to your left,' he gestured vaguely. 'I'll grab a pair of socks and be right with you.'

Billie moved further into the house and the room he suggested. Feeling uncomfortable and unable to sit, she walked to the front windows and stood with her back to the room, stiffly rubbing her crossed arms. Soft footsteps behind alerted her to his presence and she slowly turned.

He stood across the room, had barely moved beyond the door, hands on hips, weariness written all over his face and stance. 'What can I do for you?'

Billie knew she'd have to toughen her softness for the guy and use what she knew about him now to give her strength. 'I called over last night but you weren't home.'

'No, I was out till late.' He hesitated. 'That your urgent question? Checking up on me?'

Billie scoffed. 'Hardly. I've just been fooled by one man. Didn't plan on making it two.'

'Where's this going, Billie?'

Her nerves were shot so she got straight to the point. 'You've been playing with the truth.'

'Excuse me?' Noah stared her down, a glitter of resistance in his eyes.

'I thought we were friends. That I could trust you.'

'You can.'

Knee-jerk reaction. Sounded honest enough but she wasn't ready to believe him just yet. She needed more. 'Bullshit. Holly came to visit me yesterday. We went for a walk and just happened to see a float plane land on the lake.' Noah's jaw ground and those charming blue eyes turned to ice. 'Could have sworn the pilot was your twin,' she said softly.

His head tilted back and Noah pushed both

hands through his thick head of sandy hair. 'Damn,' he groaned. 'It's not how it looks and what you think.'

'You working for them?'

'Depends on who you mean by *them*. Billie, you can't get involved in this. You never saw a thing and you need to back off. Right now.' The threatening growl in his tone was warning, concern, not bitter defence. And his explanation neither sounded nor looked like he felt the least bit guilty.

'As if,' she scoffed, crossing her arms again, comfortable now the truth was out. 'You paid out Michelle and you're renovating. Do you need the money?'

'You are way off the mark.' Noah fell silent and his emotions went underground. Eventually, he threw out a heavy sigh of frustration, edged with amusement. 'You are so damn nosy it's gonna get you into a heap of trouble one day. And I'll tell you now, this time you're too damn close for your own safety.'

'I'm not like every other woman. I learned early on if I wanted to survive I had to fend for myself and make my own decisions. And FYI? In case you hadn't noticed, I can handle myself and I haven't been caught spying.'

'Yet. But you've raised suspicion and been paid a visit. You're on a watch list. From now on, Billie, despite everything you think you know, you need to trust me and stay out of this.

Otherwise I'll have to get Ewan Holt to read you the riot act. Failing that, maybe snap on some handcuffs and keep you safely locked up in the station till all this is over.'

'So what exactly is *this?* Big time stuff?'

'I won't say this again. You go back to the shack, keep your mouth shut and stay out of trouble. No more visits to the Bend, okay?' When Billie hesitated, he insisted, 'Promise!'

'Only if you tell me your involvement.'

'Sheesh, woman. I've had a serious twenty four hours undercover and just got back. This is serious business, okay?'

Undercover! He was some kind of spy? Filled with the biggest relief and amazing joy, Billie found herself nodding. 'I understand.'

'No you don't. Not yet. But you will. Look,' he stepped forward and his tone softened, 'I got back in the wee hours and I don't function till I've had a decent breakfast. You can stay and join me or watch me eat. I'll let you in on the basics,' he wagged a finger, 'but that's it. The less you know the better.'

'How can I promise if I don't know the details?'

'You don't *need* to know.' Noah shook his head and muttered, 'I'll be more agreeable after I've been fed.'

When he turned and left the room, Billie trailed after him down the hallway, feeling elated. He was doing some kind of police work.

He wasn't on the wrong side after all. But *undercover?* Didn't that suggest danger? Guns. Criminals.

With her mood having changed in a heartbeat from happiness to worry at the thought of risk to Noah, Billie hardly noticed the new floor boards he had added to the kitchen. The moment she entered the homely space she was hit by warmth from the wood stove, its firebox open. She rolled her neck and shoulders to unwind, taking a seat at a small table in one of two chairs.

Noah half turned. 'You hungry?'

Billie shook her head. 'I've already eaten.'

Buddy was stretched out beside the fire where Noah tossed strips of bacon into a pan then grabbed a long-handled fork and made toast from the glowing coals. Billie watched with simple pleasure as he cracked eggs into the pan and when his man meal was done, slid it all onto a plate and joined her at the table.

Billie left him in peace while he ate. When the kettle sang on the cast iron hob, she asked, 'Can I make you a cuppa?'

He nodded, his mouth full. She rose and went over to a small timber side table where she found tea, coffee and sugar, a bottle of milk was in an ice-filled esky alongside. She returned with two mugs of tea and set one in front of him.

Billie asked, 'Have you actually gone to Ewan Holt yet about the number plate?'

'Yeah but with a last minute change of plans thrown at us all yesterday, the local police and city investigation team were kept busy. We debriefed late. Might know more today. Probably turn out to be a fake. I've seen the vehicle from the jetty but they usually don't let me out of the plane so I can't get a close look. We need an engine number to identify the owner but that means getting to the vehicle. We have no idea where it goes.'

Billie considered his comments. 'I've seen it a few times now. Some of David's wealthy business contacts drove something similar. Could be a Range Rover.'

'Yeah, that's what we're thinking. Classy. There's money in drugs.'

As she should have known, the whole situation was well under control. 'How did you get involved in all this?'

Noah finished his breakfast, sat back and took a deep gulp of his hot tea. 'Because I'm local, I know the area. Plus I'm a pilot and military trained for ops. Middle East mostly. Military airlifts of arms and munitions. Air patrols, humanitarian aid.'

Billie was impressed and so proud of him. The average citizen had no idea the importance of every member of the defence forces. 'Holly thought the float plane was cool.' Billie grinned. 'I'm surprised our lakes around here are deep enough for one.'

Noah shrugged. 'Long as you have about half a metre below the floats when the plane is stationary and fully loaded you're fine. Learning to fly one was always near the top of my aviation bucket list. A seaplane rating opens up opportunities to explore wild remote areas of the world. Don't even need a runway.'

Billy could see by the enjoyment in his voice and on his face that he was born for such adventures.

'So this all came about from your time in the air force?'

'A few months ago, Ewan Holt asked me to come on board and help the police operation take down a drug ring that's started operating in the area. Jump on it before it developed into something bigger. They needed someone on the inside.

'After I agreed, my handlers got me inside the organisation. I've gained their confidence by doing my job, not asking questions and being reliable. Now we're familiar with their strategy of changing routes, we're putting all the pieces together.

'After I'm contacted for another run, I'm picked up and blindfolded till I get to the plane. There's a whole lot of separate sections to the organisation. Only one or two people are involved at each stage. I've never logged a flight plan. I doubt that's ever done. So there's no way the flights can be traced. Mid-flight on the trip back, I get a message with coordinates for landing. I've never returned to the same place twice.

Noah pushed out a breath of frustration. 'But we still haven't identified the local connection. Someone is feeding them information. We believe that black four wheel drive is the link. If we can nail that, we'll have someone to watch and be closer to setting up a bust.'

Noah sent Billie a loaded glance. 'To be honest, because of your presence near the drop zone, I believe the organisation is growing nervous. That's why the sudden change yesterday. If the people in charge of this whole operation get wind of even the slightest hitch, they'll pull out and we'll have lost valuable work and intelligence. To avoid that and keep you out of trouble, the ideal situation is you not being here at all. You need to get out of that shack and leave. Today.'

Despite the cosy atmosphere in the homestead, Billie grew cold at Noah's demand. 'That bad.'

Noah leant forward in his chair and reached across the small table, grasping her hands in his. 'It's not a choice, Billie. It's unsafe you're so close. It's the worst timing. They know where I live and I'm being watched. Your visits to the farm and presence in the shack have raised alarms. It's too risky now. You need to go.'

She tried to disregard the intimate touch of Noah's warm hands wrapped around hers. 'Okay. I get it. This is serious. I shouldn't be here.' After a pause, she decided to ask, 'Why did you agree to get involved in this?'

Noah released her hands and rose, taking his plate and mug to the sink. He returned to her side at the table, grabbed her hand and pulled her up in front of him. 'I lost a mate to drugs. Saw exactly what it does to a person. And he was simply one of many who served and suffered from PTSD after returning from overseas. Can be hard to forget what we've seen and done. I know another guy who's really struggling. It's a tough battle for him and I'm hoping he'll win but there's no guarantee. If I can help get some of that shit off the streets, I'll do it.'

Aware Noah was still holding her hand, his muscled body almost touching hers, Billie felt a stirring of a familiar longing for this man. Her mind went to war with her common sense. Barely weeks out from breaking up a long term relationship, how crazy to even think about letting herself get involved with another man. She simply must ignore this chemistry. Especially at the moment. They could both be in line for a whole bunch of trouble.

'Is this an ongoing thing for you?' she probed. 'Helping the police?'

He shrugged. 'I fitted their criteria this time

around. And I'm not long back from serving so maybe not a rusty old veteran yet?' He grinned.

'You'll never grow rusty. And I thought you were simply a harmless laid-back farmer. Fooled me. Wearing your daggy clothes and muddy boots.'

'I can't be all too bad on the eyes,' he drawled. 'I've caught you staring.'

'Can't help it when you're right in front of me.'

'You're holding my hand.'

'You took it.'

'Yeah, I did, didn't I? Ah, Billie Gibbs,' he breathed and let his free arm slide around her waist to draw her tight. She felt the graze of his stubble against her forehead when he brushed his lips against her skin. 'This is a bad move.'

He lowered his head, put a finger to her chin and tilted her face to meet his, pressing the gentlest sexy kiss to her mouth that washed with agonising delight through her whole body.

'When all this is over, I might just come and find you,' he murmured, drawing apart.

Lazy with yearning, Billie would have stayed and explored wonderful things with this man. What a tease. How dare he kiss like that when she was leaving? As payback, she said softly, 'I might not want to be found.'

'I'm a country man. I could find you in the dark without GPS. I know my directions and I never get lost,' he growled.

'Never?'

'Thought doesn't appeal?'

'Guess you'll just have to wait and see.'

He stepped back, creating distance to make her leaving easier? Billie also noticed he thrust his hands into his pockets. To keep them from misbehaving? And was looking far too gorgeous to leave behind. But there it was. The moment had come. Much sooner than she expected and in circumstances beyond anything either of them could control.

With the hardest effort, she turned and walked back down the hallway toward the front door. It hurt when she didn't hear any following footsteps.

'I have your number.'

Billie's pace faltered and his soft words put a smile on her face, but parting left another scar on her heart for the unknown days and weeks ahead.

Chapter 7

Against her strongest instincts to hang around the lake and watch the coming events unfold, Billie sped back to the shack, feeling a sense of urgency from Noah's revelations. Anxious for *his* safety more than her own now. She could get away but he was staying in dangerous circumstances. Her idyllic and remarkable breather in the shack was coming to an end.

Who knew that her lakeside hideaway would come to mean something altogether different from its original purpose?

Before heading indoors to pack, Billie allowed herself a few last precious moments to stand on the deck and absorb her surroundings. The lake's still glassy surface throwing back reflections. The twittering and screeching of birds in the trees, echoing across the water. Ducks flapping and splashing among the reeds. The gentle air of peace that surrounded you if you simply stood and watched and listened.

What had she gained from these past ten days? Ignoring plane and drone interruptions, and the distraction of a certain local farmer who sure knew how to combine a first and goodbye kiss into one, leaving a woman reeling. She held onto the hope that Noah would get in touch when his part in the current police operation was over.

Much more basically, she took comfort that his attraction had grown from seeing her vulnerable and natural, not trying to impress. Afraid on reflection and to her shame that, since meeting David, she had been guilty of being drawn into another world, influenced by its temptations and promises. Believing she wanted it herself. Where friends betrayed and money ruled.

An unreal world as she now saw it. Which she no longer wanted. At least she had worked out that much. If not necessarily where and how her future lay. Encouraged, knowing there *were* decent people out there. Ordinary maybe but genuine, content. Honest.

And of course those thoughts all comprised Noah Sutton.

Time apart from him would be difficult, subtle torment. She would miss him. Until she learned he was safe. Distance from the lake and shack to which she had run was now crucial to avoid potential danger as the police investigation escalated. Wisely or not, she had allowed herself to be drawn into the charisma of a rugged handsome man, and involved herself in other matters, not knowing how serious the situation. Both activities allowing her to avoid facing the troubles from which she had fled yet placing her in danger. One of the heart and the other of her life.

Down the track, keeping in touch would be up to Noah. She was born here but lived all her adult life so far in Melbourne. At the moment, Billie knew since returning home she was now torn between the two worlds and what each offered. Still lots to consider and decide but she had made a start. Forced away, for now, from unwanted circumstances.

Not exactly the reflective peaceful break she imagined but nonetheless rewarding. In small ways, revealing. Challenging her mind and hopes. Making new friends in Noah and Holly. She would stop by the roadhouse and say a quick hello on her way back to the city. The return trip not the happiest thought but she had an old life to wind up and her future to reassess.

Speaking of which, Billie sighed, she must get to it.

Moving inside, she gathered the carry bags and boxes she had stored in a cupboard since her arrival and began packing up her foodstuffs in the kitchenette.

Billie was just in the process of tackling her clothes in the bedroom when she heard an all too familiar rumbling motor. She stilled. The black four wheel drive. A complication of the worst kind. It had to be someone connected with the drug organisation. Damn, she swore softly, wishing she hadn't wasted time out on the deck. Was she too late? Was this it? There was certainly no escape route to her car without being seen.

Billie hurriedly threw blankets over her packing and closed the bedroom door. As she walked through the living area, she eyed the other boxes and moaned. Too late to hide them because footsteps already sounded out on the deck. She would just have to try and keep her visitor from coming inside the shack. Billie pulled the door behind her as she stepped out to meet her fate.

And faltered in shock.

Once she adjusted to the changes, she soon recognised the young man strolling toward her. A slightly taller leggy blonde in a short and tight leather skirt, skimpy tank top and cropped denim jacket, barely old enough to have finished high school Billie would have thought, possessively clung to his arm. Staking her claim to the wealthy son.

Up close and remembering that inevitable smirk curling up the corners of his mouth, Billie realised how much Mason Lowe Jnr had altered since their days around the school yard as kids. He had put on weight.

She was not only surprised by Mason's physical decline, product of his fast lifestyle, no doubt. It also struck her that, if he was driving the black four wheel drive, was *he* the owner?

Made sense. Lowe's had money. Mason Jnr always preened when showing off any proof of his family's prosperity. Luxury car. Trophy sex symbol on his arm.

If so, that placed him right in the thick of the drug ring. And it was probably no accident that he should be here right around the time of yesterday's sudden drug drop.

So, if Mason was involved and had previously been informed about Billie staying in the shack near Willow Bend jetty, her questionable presence and every movement so far would already have been passed on to him.

This was not a social call. This was all about business and checking up on her. God, she hoped he didn't push his way inside to see the scattered mess around the shack. He would know she was leaving. If he didn't want that to happen, he might try to stop her.

Billie's anxiety level shot up but she knew she had to play this cool. Force herself to be friendly, look surprised.

Knowing he would hate the description, she gushed, 'I don't believe it. Sasha's baby brother.'

Mason cast her a steady glare. 'Saw a blue car coming from the direction of the Sutton place as I drove in. Came to make sure there were no trespassers in the shack.'

A bare-faced lie. He knew she would be here and was up to his chubby little ears in it all.

Billie played along. 'So you haven't spoken to your sister recently, then?'

His gaze narrowed. 'What's Sash got to do with anything?'

'Since the shack is always empty this time of year, she suggested I come out here and stay for a while. We're in touch every day. She's probably just forgotten to mention it to anyone else in the family.' Billie decided on one other test and pulled her mobile from her pocket. 'I can call your father if you like. Confirm it's okay I'm here?'

If Mason Snr wasn't involved in all this, Junior sure wouldn't want him knowing about it.

'No need,' he flashed back. Then, always on the lookout for a slur, he added unkindly, 'Yeah, I heard your ladder-climbing fiancé ditched you.'

Billie flinched. Is that how some people saw David?

'Come out here to lick your wounds?' he sneered.

Billie clenched her hands into fists at her side to stop herself from landing a kick in that smug face and plastered on a fake smile instead.

'I'm taking a break, yes. Noah has made me feel welcome. I've appreciated his friendship. Like you, he came calling to make sure all was well here at the shack. He didn't know I was here either. I'm sure your family would want a neighbour to watch out for their property.'

She hoped that covered being in Noah's company to Junior's satisfaction and that no conspiracy was involved in their friendship. If she had been watched, she couldn't hide her visits and connection with Noah while she had been staying here. So she didn't try. Best to be up front and set the record straight with the truth. Field any misconceptions this little upstart might have. Whatever his place in the hierarchy. Surely if the organisation held suspicions about their friendship, Noah would have been confronted by now?

Mason didn't look pleased to be corrected and, judging by his narrowed glare, only reluctantly convinced by her explanation. He switched his hard stare from Billie and glanced with possessive pride at the girl hugging him close. 'This is my fiancé, Hailey. We'll be staying at the farmhouse a few nights.'

Billie's heart kicked into overdrive. Best and worst news ever. The nasty little turd would be just across the paddock but, she grew suddenly excited about the unbelievable opportunity this presented. If only these two young things would leave so she could set wheels in motion to accomplish it.

She couldn't resist one last dig. 'Wouldn't have thought the country was your favourite place anymore, Mason.'

'It's not.' His beady eyes kept flashing about, checking everything around them.

'Intriguing.' Billie crossed her arms, enjoying the banter. 'Can't be business way out here.' She paused for effect knowing it was exactly that. '*Private* time with your young lady?' she teased, grinning at Hailey.

Who totally missed the point if the unsmiling expression and ice blue eyes were any indication. Okay, not amused.

'Showing Hailey the ancestral family homestead,' he boasted.

Not a romantic tropical island? Why here? Billie almost laughed in his faced. Mason's father was a city investor who had bought the property, share farmed it so someone else did all the work, stuck it out living in the house with his family for a decade then leased out the entire concern and moved back to Melbourne. Whereas most of the landowners around here had handed down their farms for generations. Like the gorgeous old house Noah was restoring, she thought idly. Now there was a true family tradition.

'I'm sure she'll be impressed.'

She was being flippant, of course. These two urban yuppies would be lucky to last the forty eight hours before high tailing it back to their urban society comforts. All the same, she wondered at the real reason for this visit which was surely connected to the drugs. And why

Mason Jnr had perhaps foolishly shown himself when, up to now, his identity and part in the local illegal activity remained carefully hidden.

Personally, Billie considered the reckless move a poor lack of judgement. Too much confidence this close to the end game? There would be so much at stake here to lose if he was caught. Which she thrilled to believe would happen soon.

Billie grew impatient for them to leave. The alarm bells that had started ringing at first sight of Mason, were growing louder. She needed to contact Noah, warn him and share their lucky chance.

As the young couple turned and walked away, Billie followed, peering around the corner of the shack to confirm it was the same vehicle. Bingo.

She waited only long enough to make sure they were well out of sight before grabbing her car keys and speeding to the Sutton farm. Praying having this information and acting on it wasn't a setup, a trap, darting glances in her mirrors to make sure she wasn't followed.

'Miss me already?'

As Billie scrambled from her car, the surprise and pleasure on Noah's face was priceless. Billie locked the image in her heart, shaking her head. Honestly, the timing of meeting this gorgeous man really sucked. But she was in a hurry and raced up the steps to meet him on the veranda. The alarm in her eyes and serious expression caught his attention.

'I think the black four wheel drive belongs to Mason Lowe Jnr and he's in it up to his neck.' She stood before him, breathless. 'He's staying on their property in the house for two nights.'

'And how do you know all this?'

'He came to the shack not five minutes ago. You know what this means? We can get the engine number to prove it.' When Noah hesitated, Billie gasped, 'We should go now.'

'Hold on a minute.' He was too calm and composed, gently taking her arm and leading her inside back down to the kitchen. 'We're not going now in broad daylight. Besides we should report this information to Ewan Holt and let the police handle it.'

'But he's right across the paddock! He's there now. And if his sexy chicklet is any indication, I doubt he'll be leaving that house any time soon,' she said wryly. 'If you get my drift.'

'It's too risky.'

From his uncertain tone of voice, Billie sensed he wasn't protesting all that hard. 'Don't tell me you're not up for a little adrenalin rush? Come on. You have the skills to do this,' she pleaded. 'I know a back way in along the creek. The ground is lower there. Even if Mason Jnr was looking he wouldn't see us approach.'

When Noah hesitated, Billie knew she had him thinking. 'We could be over there, have this mission done and the information passed on to the police within an hour.'

Noah's jaw worked while he paced and she knew she had him thinking. 'I'll keep watch at the house,' Billie offered, 'while you go get the number from the vehicle. We'll put our phones on silent and I'll text if it looks like he's leaving the house.'

'The vehicle might be locked.'

Billie tilted her head to the side and raised her eyebrows in despair. 'I'm willing to bet you've met way tougher problems than that.'

Noah crossed his arms and slowly shook his head. 'This is so wrong on all fronts.'

'But you're tempted? We're doing this, right?'

'Sheesh woman, I thought I was rid of you. Sent you away for your own safety. Now you're back and dragging us both into it again. Getting involved way over your head.'

Billie grinned at his friendly ribbing. 'Not this time. If we go in along the river and come up behind the farm sheds, we'll have cover practically the whole way in.'

'Okay, I'll do it.' He held up a hand to stem Billie's squeak of joy. 'But I'm going in with a piece. You stay out of sight and do as I say.' She nodded. 'Your phone charged and on you?'

'Yep.'

'Can you drive a small farm motorbike?'

'Used to be able to. Why?'

'I have one and it will make less noise than either your car or my ute. We'll take that. Easier to go off road across country if we need to avoid anyone chasing us. I'll tie up Buddy so he doesn't follow and give us away.'

When Noah was sorted at the homestead, Billie trailed after him across the yard to a small outbuilding. He unlocked a metal cabinet in one corner, pulled out a hand gun and bike keys before locking it again.

At Billie's wide-eyed gaze on the weapon, Noah said, 'Only for an emergency. It's not loaded. Might come in handy as a threat.'

To practise her rusty motor bike skills and because she knew the way, Noah let Billie drive the bike down toward the creek, following a grassy track along its banks until they were behind the Lowe house.

The feel of his big arms around her and his body pressed hard up against her back, filled her with a thrill even greater than the thought of what they were about to do. Trespass onto a neighbouring property, steal an engine number and escape. Simple.

When they grew closer, Noah signalled her to shut off the engine. They legged it off the bike and left it hidden. Again, since Billie was familiar with the layout of the property from farm visits here as kids before Sasha and her family moved back to the city, she led Noah between old sheds and outbuildings, closer to the house.

The black four wheel drive was parked outside in front of the garage. Right out in the open in broad daylight. They glanced at each other. The vehicle was fully exposed and visible from any one of the many house windows.

When Billie began moving away, Noah hissed, 'What are you doing?'

'Getting closer to the house. I'll hear if they're talking and sound like they might leave. I can warn you.'

He scowled. 'Be careful.'

'You too. Good luck.'

Keeping low, Billie jogged behind the cover of garden shrubs toward the house, heading for the patio and its double sliding doors between the living area at one end and the bedroom wing at the other. The most likely way Mason would come out to access his vehicle.

Billie heard voices from inside. One voice actually. Mason. In case the discussion revealed valuable information, she moved forward and peered in. All she saw was the backs of two heads seated on a sofa. Even risking an ear to the window, she couldn't clearly make out what he was saying. She knelt on the ground and slowly slid the door ajar a fraction.

Although his voice was low, his words were just audible.

'Honestly babe, I'm fed up with being a city guy in a suit and taking orders from the old man. I hate the goddam office and the family business and everything in it.'

Hailey murmured something that sounded like sympathy and they kissed.

'Just one more night, babe. All our planning has paid off. One last shipment day after tomorrow. Then we can ditch this country and go live a life of freedom and luxury overseas.'

'I can't wait.' Hailey sounded innocent and breathless.

'Either can I, babe.' He drew her against him and they disappeared from sight down onto the sofa. Lying flat on the ground outside the slightly open door, Billie grinned in amusement.

'Not here,' Hailey giggled.

When they surfaced higher up on the sofa again and rose, Billie swiftly shuffled further backwards out of sight. She flashed a quick glance out to the yard where Noah was squatted in front of the vehicle and trying to prize open the bonnet with some kind of levering instrument. He must have found it in a shed. Turning her attention back to the lovebirds in the house, she didn't miss the next snippet of conversation because their voices grew louder and closer.

'Bedroom,' Mason growled.

'I need my things,' she whined, 'and my case is still in the car.'

'We don't need clothes.'

'Please baby.'

'Okay but you start getting undressed.'

Billie scuttled around the corner of the house and sent off a warning text to Noah. She had no idea where he went because next thing she knew he had disappeared out of sight the other side of the bushes.

Meanwhile, Mason must have emerged through the partly-open sliding door because his footsteps echoed on the paving as he crossed. Then she heard the crunch of gravel and a beep as he remotely unlocked the vehicle and was probably unloading their cases.

Billie held her breath, hoping Noah had time and a place to hide. Mason's returning footsteps approached the house again and, just before the sliding door slammed shut, she heard the beep of the four wheel drive being remotely locked again. She slid down to the ground, her back to the house brick wall. Noah must be safe.

She only hoped Mason and his girlfriend took their time in the bedroom because, last she glimpsed, Noah still hadn't opened the bonnet. Having gathered more information and trusting the young couple were happily occupied for a while, Billie crouched low again behind the bushes scrambling back toward the car.

To her relief, Noah was kneeling before the vehicle again prying a screwdriver in through the grille until she heard him slide the bonnet latch and pop it free.

'Hold it open,' he murmured.

He fished his mobile from his pocket, turned on its flashlight, leaned across the engine and she heard the shutter click as he took a photo. He slid upright again, gently closed the bonnet, grabbed Billie's hand and they ran.

They rested against the side of a corrugated iron shed near the motor bike to catch their breath.

'Mason said something was on at first light day after tomorrow then they're escaping the country.'

'Probably South America,' Noah muttered. Tapping out quickly on his phone, he sent off a text about Billie's new message and the engine number photo to Ewan Holt. 'He's gonna have some questions about our methods but he'll get over it. This should set up his team for a bust. And I figure I'm about to get a call to fly the plane again.'

They rode back to the homestead, edgy but rewarded from their scouting mission. Noah cracked a beer for both of them.

'It's not even midday yet,' Billie chuckled, clinking their ice-cold bottles together.

'You did good,' he drawled. 'With this intel about Mason's involvement, the police will upgrade their surveillance on him and the drop site at the lake. You packed yet?'

Sounded heartless but reality set in again. Billie had to leave. She nodded. 'Almost. Shouldn't take long.'

'If the bust goes ahead when Mason says, I'll be missing for a few days.' He shrugged. 'Might be 48 hours. Don't panic. I have my backup team, okay?'

Billie nodded, putting on a brave outward face but inwardly terrified for him. Then told herself he was ex-military, he'd seen bigger action and he would have support. All the same, she couldn't help the spread of anxiety that paralysed her mind and body.

Perhaps noticing her tension, Noah said warmly, 'Don't hang about. Get moving. Head back to the city and make yourself scarce. No telling how far this organisation will go to deal with anyone they believe may be trouble. Don't use your phone. Don't tell Sasha Lowe or anyone where you are. Keep your distance and keep to yourself.'

'For how long?'

'Until you hear from me.'

'And how will that happen if I can't use my phone,' she bantered.

He leaned close, brushed the hair aside from her face and softly whispered a code word into her ear. Before transferring his gorgeous mouth to hers for yet another scorching goodbye.

And this time it *was* final. At least for a while.

Chapter 8

It was almost midday when Billie returned to the shack to finish the packing she had begun earlier. Before Mason Junior's surprise visit, which then meant a drive over to tell Noah of their opportunity and do something about it.

Getting the engine number from the black four wheel drive at the Lowe property had been tricky but successful. Now it simply remained for the police to use the information in helping bring their investigation to a successful result.

In the middle of frantically stuffing her belongings into bags, boxes and her suitcase, Billie grew aware of creaking. Sounded like it was coming from the deck. Cautiously, she crept from the bedroom, slowly peering around the hall doorway into the living area.

Next thing she knew she had been thrown to the floor. It happened so fast she had no time to react. If attacked, her taekwondo self-defence training had taught her to stay calm and not panic. To keep on thinking despite the circumstances. Easily said. She'd never had to put it into practise before. She did now.

As a masked man towered above her aiming

a gun, Billie shuffled her body until she faced him, bent her knees and kicked him hard. He stumbled backward and the gun flew from his hand, giving her enough time to scramble to her feet. She took up a fighting stance and prepared to take him on. At least now without the weapon, the contest would be on more equal terms.

As he straightened and recovered, lunging at her, Billie raised her knee and straightened her leg, aiming for his head with a foot kick. Grunting and off balance, the guy stumbled back against the wall.

She hadn't expected him to give up. Recovering, he charged her again so she repeated the kick. The guy was unstoppable, reeling, then circled and reached out to grab her wrist. She used her free arm to push him back hard with her hand under his chin. Her knee to his torso bent him double so she pushed him down and gave a sharp hand strike to the side of his neck.

Stunned, he dropped flat to the floor. Billie kicked the gun further away and grabbed a tea towel, quickly tying his hands behind his back in tight knots enough to disable him so she could get away.

A search of his pockets found a set of car keys and a mobile. Together with the gun, she threw them all into the lake. While the attacker growled behind his mask and struggled, Billie grabbed her stuff and loaded it into her car.

The guy would probably work his hands free soon but at least her basic efforts would slow him before he had a chance to follow. Billie turned off her phone for safety against any tracking signal. Before she drove away, she took a few precious minutes to search under her car and around the wheels in case a tracking device had been planted, but found nothing.

As her SUV sped away from the shack and across the paddock toward the main road, her mind was still not at ease in case she missed any device on her vehicle. They had threatened her the first time, just now tried to put her out of action and would probably try again. But they had to find and catch her first.

Once she turned onto the highway heading south to the city, her morning's actions and the last attacking encounter all hit home on her emotions. To reduce her pounding heart and shaking, she took in deep breaths, gripped the steering wheel tighter but kept on driving. She needed to be off the highway and hidden as soon as possible.

Noah had advised returning to Melbourne immediately but she felt no rush to go back. It felt too far away from him. So she decided to ignore his suggestion and instead drove to the Coach Roadhouse and pulled into a park at the rear.

It nagged her that she had wanted to call in and see her mother, Heather, back in town. With so much happening and the urgency to escape, she would put that visit on hold for a few days until this current upheaval was sorted and Noah returned safe.

Holly was pleasantly surprised to see her and beamed as she approached the counter. 'Hey Billie.'

'I need your help.'

She anxiously scanned the restaurant, not knowing what to look for or what she expected to find but fear travelled with her now and she figured she wouldn't know peace until she was safely in hiding and heard from Noah.

Holly's attention sharpened 'Of course, you have it. What do you want me to do?'

'You rent cabins out the back. I'd like to reserve one for a few days before I return to Melbourne.'

'Sure. I'll get Gracie. She usually does the bookings.'

Holly made to go and find her boss but Billie reached across the counter and grasped her arm. 'Does she need to know?'

'Yes. She and Sid take all the accommodation bookings.' Holly leaned forward, frowning. 'Does this have anything to do with that morning at the lake?'

Billie nodded.

'Relax. You can trust them.'

Where Billie had been Holly's backstop and reassurance days ago, now her friend returned the favour.

'Wait here.'

Moments later, colourful Gracie appeared, her mane of thick grey hair floating about her face and shoulders, complemented by her trademark red-framed glasses. With calmness and a familiar ready smile, she said, 'Billie, follow me.'

Relieved to have someone else take control, she did as she was told. In Gracie's office, once the door was safely shut, the older woman gently urged her down into a chair and poured a brandy.

'Sip this and tell me what you need.'

Billie coughed over the first sharp mouthful. 'I need a place to hide my car and myself for a few days. I don't want to see anyone and I don't want anyone to see me. I need to be invisible.'

Gracie grinned, rose and patted her hand. 'Consider it done. Wait here, finish your brandy and I'll arrange it.'

Waiting alone, the thought flashed through Billie's mind that she wished her mother could have been as competent and assured as Gracie. In a few days, when all this drug business was hopefully over, she would sit down and have a long overdue chat with Heather. Scope out the living circumstances with her father, Jack, and see what needed to be done. If anything.

Personally, Billie believed it was way past the time Heather took a stand and dealt with what she considered her broken life. Billie planned to put some cold hard facts in front of her mother. Maybe she would back away and choose to stay with her husband but the compliant woman needed to know she had support if she decided otherwise.

It was obvious the siblings that had stayed around town had neither helped their mother nor done anything to improve her situation. Billie was sure that, between them all, they could work out something.

She was only just growing to realise how much personal happiness meant in this world. Not money or climbing to the top rung of the career ladder. Sure, some craved it. Once, Billie had, too. No more.

Meredith had done well in the legal profession, by choice, to help others and because she loved it. It was clearly her calling in life. Her baby sister didn't want or need to prove anything to anybody except to make the most of her life in the manner that made her content.

Billie realised that she hadn't sat down like this, with or without the influence of some good French brandy, according to the label on the bottle, and really given her life and family much consideration in recent years.

Time for many revelations, it seemed. Maybe David did her more of a favour than she appreciated since he was the catalyst for much that had changed in her life over the past month.

In recent weeks, Billie had slowly grown to understand why she was suddenly analysing family. Now her long term relationship with David was over, she questioned why it hadn't worked. Simple fact was, she and David each wanted entirely different things from their lives.

Since returning to her hometown and the lake shack with its simple surroundings and peace, the *country* part of her had risen to become stronger than she could ever have imagined. Lying hidden until she discovered for herself it was what she needed.

Being honest, that shift was largely influenced by meeting Noah. Knowing an immediate intrigue and attraction to an earthy man of the land. A completely opposite personality and appeal from her few other city liaisons. Although there had been that one time after the high school graduation dance where a farming lad had shown her a thing or two…

Billie smiled in reflection.

'You're looking better,' Gracie announced as she bustled back into her office.

'Sitting still and brandy worked. I've been deep in contemplation.'

'Always a good thing.' Gracie perched on the end of her desk and dangled a set of keys. 'You're in cabin ten right at the end of the accommodation wing. Lots of privacy down there.'

Billie took the keys. 'Thank you. Can I pay you in cash?' After going to all this trouble she didn't want to risk being traced.

'Of course. When you leave is soon enough, dear. I'll tell the girls to keep a tab for you. Just phone reception to order your meals and anything else you need.'

Billie rose, filled with gratitude. People like Holly and Gracie and Noah all restored your faith in humanity. 'Gracie, I can't thank you enough.'

'You're welcome. If you give me your car keys, I'll garage it in a spare locked shed out the back.'

'I'll need my suitcase first.'

'I'll fetch it for you.'

'Oh. Great.' Billie fished in her shoulder bag and handed them over.

'I'll walk you out through the back way where it's more private.'

'You haven't asked me why,' Billie queried as they strolled together along the veranda that ran the length of the cabins.

'Don't need to know, dear. None of my business. I've known you all your life.'

'It's serious and important,' Billie felt compelled to explain.

'Wouldn't expect otherwise.'

To her pleasure at first sight, cabin ten was a glamorous modern version of the shack. A clean respite for weary travellers. Soft comfortable bed, she discovered, sitting on it. Gleaming bathroom. No five minute showers here. And a new coffee pod machine. Glancing around the spacious country suite, it was clear in this simple room she had everything she needed.

Then it hit her. The aftermath of recent weeks, especially recent days when the plane and drug activity had increased, and its fallout had impacted her life. With threats from pompous little upstarts that looked like Mason Jnr and nasty assaults from thugs and strangers. Tears pooled in her eyes and rolled down her cheeks. She was here and safe, thanks to the kindness of friends.

Now all that remained was to set eyes on Noah again, handsome and all in one piece, and her world would be complete.

Taking her time to emotionally recover and making use of a box of tissues by the bed, Billie rose and peeled off her clothes to indulge in a long hot shower. Afterwards, she drew the curtains, sank onto the bed and fell asleep.

When Billie woke around dusk, her case had been delivered. She turned on the television and ordered in her evening meal.

Holly delivered it but only stayed for a moment. 'I'm in Cabin One up the other end. The room closest to the main building.'

Holly eyed her closely but thankfully left her alone. Time for a chat tomorrow.

Incredibly, Billie turned off the television and slept again. Breakfast arrived, then lunch later, each time with a knock on the door. She waited a while before she cautiously answered it, the staff having already disappeared. Billie sensed staying anonymous was the key.

Waiting was beyond difficult. More like agonising. Patience was never her strength. She just needed to get through the next two nights and days but at least, by staying in the area, she was closer to Noah when he contacted her again. And in case anything happened, but she chose not to dwell on that prospect.

That evening, unable to resist any longer, Billie flicked on her phone but only for seconds. Enough to see if there was any code message from Noah, though she didn't expect it yet.

Half an hour earlier, she noticed, Holly had sent a text *Want company?*

Billie responded *Y*. Then immediately turned off her phone again.

When Holly arrived, although she doubted there was any need, Billie swore her friend to secrecy and briefly related the basics of the events that had unfolded in recent days.

'There's been nothing on the television news,' Holly said. 'We keep it on all day in the restaurant for travellers.'

'Yeah, I've been checking, too. In between trying to concentrate on a bit of reading. Hopefully I'll hear something tomorrow.'

After another restless night and long tedious day, when Billie briefly switched on her phone again toward evening without any word from Noah, she grew more than concerned. If the police raid had taken place, they were keeping it quiet because there was nothing on the television or local radio news. It was more than 48 hours. Noah should have been in touch by now, surely?

Billie could barely force down her dinner and barely slept the following night. Next morning, she decided to hell with staying out of sight. She was going to find Noah.

Chapter 9

'I think you should stay put,' Holly warned, as she reluctantly handed over the car keys.

Billie shook her head and gave her friend a quick hug. 'Can't.'

'Those guys aren't playing around.'

'I know. But there hasn't been any news. Either nothing happened or something did but things went wrong.'

'The police will deal with all that. Can't you be patient for one more day?'

'Nope.'

Holly slowly shook her head, her expression filled with doubt and she said seriously, 'In the first days after my mother went missing, I got this really bad feeling. I'm getting the same thing now. Please don't go.'

Billie stopped packing her shoulder bag to reassure her nervous friend. 'I'm just going to look. I'll be careful. Don't worry, I'll be back.'

'You don't know that.' Holly nervously rubbed her arms. 'Gracie's mad.'

Billie grinned and slung her bag over a shoulder. 'I can imagine. I'll be in touch as soon as I can.'

As Billie climbed into her car and started it up for the first time in days, unsure whether to keep her phone off or flick it on, she couldn't help sharing some of Holly's reservations. But the force to go investigate was too strong. No harm in scouting around to see what was happening.

Turning out onto the highway, she decided to do the right thing and start at the police station first. She might gain some small piece of reassuring news or leave disheartened. Naturally, she hoped it was positive but prepared herself to be disappointed.

It couldn't be worse than the past few days. Endless, useless thoughts kept swirling through her head until Billie felt it might burst.

Had the drug drop been pushed forward and gone ahead earlier than Mason Jnr claimed? Was it already over and the police didn't have a chance for the raid? In that case, if the drug drop went ahead and Noah wasn't part of it, he should be around or with the police. If he *was* part of it as a pilot flying the float plane, where was he? Were the organisation still holding him for some reason? Was he injured or had something nasty done to him? Was his cover blown?

Parking in front of the station later, Billie prepared herself and went inside. The female officer at the front desk greeted her with a smile.

'Is Ewan Holt available?'

'I'm sorry. He's not in the station at the moment.'

'Can you tell me anything about the drug bust?'

As Billie expected, the officer remained solemn and professional. 'I can't comment on official police business or any ongoing investigations.'

'I just need to know where my friend is,' Billie pleaded. 'Noah Sutton? He's working with the police.'

'I'm sorry I can't help you. I suggest you be patient and go home. I'm sure your friend will be in touch when he can.'

'Well I'm not,' Billie muttered, irritated at the expected response, having prepared herself to be discouraged but not liking it. 'You don't know that any more than I do.'

'Didn't these people care?' Billie grumbled, as she strode from the police station, her brain churning over where to go next. She would simply start at the beginning. Which found her heading out of town toward Reedy Lake.

Billie had returned to many places in her life but pulling up outside the shack brought her the strongest sense of déjà-vu. Stepping from her car and wandering guardedly around onto the front deck, the waters that stretched out before her and which she had left only days before, seemed like a place from another lifetime. As if another person had lived those weeks here. Perhaps, even after such a short period of time, she *had* been.

Where previously she had come for sanctuary and begun her life's transition to its next stage, discovering two precious new friendships in Noah and Holly, today she found nothing. Only still reflections, the familiar sounds of the lake's resident birds, the ducks as always sailing and squawking among the reeds.

Aware this time she was probably trespassing and not knowing where the coming months and years would lead, Billie also knew she would love to regularly return here. Continue a tradition of simplicity and escape. Not necessarily from anything in particular but purely for her soul. She acknowledged she hadn't been true to herself since leaving the country. One of many things that would change in her life.

Because it had been such a pivotal spot during her stay here, Billie strode out around the lake bushland to Willow Bend jetty. Even before she reached it, she detected that the peace of the shack where she had stood alone before was about to be interrupted here by busy human presence.

Crime scene tape stretched around the perimeter and also cordoned off the lake jetty, including the float plane, barring all access. Vehicles and police officers bustled about their duties. Something must have gone down. Why then had Noah not returned?

No point in asking questions. Billie assumed they would only be diverted like her experience at the police station in town. Interesting to see the black four wheel drive and the other familiar utes being searched and photographed by teams of investigators.

The activity left a hollow pit in Billie's stomach. It suggested a successful raid that had not yet, for some mysterious reason, made its way onto any media sources and did not explain Noah's absence.

On her way to the Sutton farm, Billie decided to drive down to the Lowe property but access was denied here, too, at the road gate by police. If the place was under wraps and being searched, that meant the authorities probably knew about Mason Jnr and his involvement. Billie didn't believe he would have risked taking part but had he been implicated, caught and arrested? Or had he kept his distance, gathered up the spoils of his drug operation and disappeared?

In a last ditch effort, Billie drove to Noah's farm. She suspected this would prove pointless because a quick check of her phone briefly turned on for the purpose confirmed still no message from Noah. She knew it was unlikely she would find him there. If he was free, he would have sent her a code so they could be in touch.

She swiftly brushed aside the thought that he did not intend to make contact again. His last goodbyes had not conveyed that impression. Quite the opposite in fact. They had been utterly loving and promising.

True enough, the property proved quiet and deserted. At least of human presence. His Merino flock grazed undisturbed on pasture, the growth lush from great winter rains. The poultry scratched and clucked in their yard but Buddy was nowhere to be seen. Billie knew a niggling concern for Noah's companion but sensed that his master would have made arrangements for his care before he left for any length of time. For a brief moment when she first stepped from her car, Billie imagined she heard Buddy's bark but when she listened again, she heard nothing.

Clutching at the last straw she could think of, Billie just wandered up the steps into the old homestead. Her footsteps echoed around the empty house as she checked each room. His belongings were still in the bedroom and clean dishes left to drain on the sink in the kitchen.

Walking back through the house, Billie stood on the front veranda gazing out around the property, praying the man she was hoping to find would simply come sauntering into sight. He would smile, walk ever closer across the yard and climb the steps…

'*Why haven't you been in touch?*' Billie murmured to herself, despair increasing with every moment. If the drug operation was busted and the jetty and the Lowe place were all under police control now, where was Noah? What was he doing? In hiding?

The remote possibility pushed her to keep looking around all the sheds and outbuildings on Noah's place. She headed first for Buddy's kennel to find his dishes full of food and water but the animal not on his chain. Billie frowned. Strange.

On instinct, she called out, 'Buddy? Hey Buddy, you here?' Thinking she heard a muffled sound from the next machinery shed, Billie slowly approached. Peering around the corner of the long open building that housed Noah's small tractor, cage animal trailer and motor bike, she tried again, 'Buddy? Hey boy, where are you?'

Casting her gaze about carefully before she moved further in, Billie slowly stepped along the side of the tractor toward the rear. She followed the soft whining that sounded like it came from a back corner. 'Buddy?'

Her low-voiced enticement drew another whimper. As she came around the end of the tractor, Buddy was lying on the floor. Billie dropped to her knees beside him.

'Hey, Buddy. What's wrong? What are you doing in here?' She ran her hands over him but didn't see or feel any sign of an injury or mishap. The beautiful animal seemed dazed, without energy. 'How did you get free from your chain? What's happened, huh?'

Even as she spoke low and stroked the dog, he raised his head from the floor and tried to bark, his eyes channelled some place behind her. Billie shut her eyes for a moment as the situation registered and she realised she had been led into a trap.

She hadn't heard anyone approach from behind and prepared herself for a defence move. This time because she had her back turned and was on the floor, the other person had every advantage.

At the awareness of another presence and slight sound of laboured breathing, she barely managed to turn around and lunge for the legs to put her attacker off balance before she felt a sharp blow to the back of her head and screamed. The piercing pain lasted mere seconds because her world went black.

Billie became semi-conscious again, aware of being half carried and dragged from the shed, then lying on the back seat bumping along in a vehicle. Confused from the nasty blow, she thought she heard Noah's voice. Which was crazy. He wouldn't have attacked or kidnapped her.

She was vaguely aware of being moved from the vehicle and indoors. She must have fallen asleep because she woke to find that her restrained world was dark because she wore a blindfold and was sitting in a chair. Her hands were tied behind her back and her head pounded with a thumping pain. Listening for any sounds, all she heard was the murmur of low voices somewhere nearby.

When a door scraped open, Billie hung her head again, pretending she was still asleep. Booted footsteps came closer and a hand roughly shook her on the shoulder.

Someone muttered, 'We must be the only two that got away. Found her lurking around your farm, man. She knows something. We need to get rid of her.'

Billie's heart jolted at the threatening comment and the suggestion that Noah was in on this. Her mind sharpened when a familiar voice replied.

'I'm a local and I don't recognise her. She's that city chick I heard was staying in the shack. Too stupid to know she was in the middle of all this. Probably came over needing help with something. Manny, you jumped her from behind, right?'

'Yeah.'

'She didn't see you?'

'Course not. Bitch didn't know what hit her.'

'Then leave her tied up,' Noah reasoned. 'She won't be able to tell the police anything.'

'If they find us, we could use her as a trade,' the other guy argued.

Billie heard what sounded like the click of a safety catch on a gun and held her breath. If the other guy didn't kill her, Noah might. He would certainly have a piece of her. All this was her fault for putting herself in harm's way. She was supposed to leave the district and head back to the city.

'First up, mate, they won't find us. Not with me leading the way. Second, no point using that gun. Waste of a bullet. Makes no sense to bring her along as a hostage. She'll just hold us back and slow us down. Come on, we gotta make tracks and get out of here. This sure was a hiccup we didn't need.'

'There's choppers and dogs out everywhere.'

'I know this country. We'll avoid them. No one will find this ruin or the girl for ages. Been deserted for years since an old timer died. No one comes here. It's a long drive in from the main road through that scrub. We'll be able to use it for cover.'

Billie guessed from the firm bravado and easy persuasion in his tone, he was playing along for their mutual survival and maintaining his cover. Also, by naming the man who just admitted to knocking her out, Noah was sending her a signal. Listen up. She might be blindfolded but her ears weren't covered. And from his description of this location, she believed she knew exactly where she was.

Holding her breath, hoping the urgency in Noah's voice against not committing murder was enough to convince the other guy.

'Come on, Manny. You planning to get arrested right here? Don't be crazy. The cops will hear a shot and be right on us. We need to split.'

Billie heard the disapproving growl of the other guy, then the thump and scraping of boots as though the men were leaving.

From outside she heard Noah say, 'You get a fix on where the choppers are at. I'll go check the ropes on that woman. Think one of them might be loose.'

When he returned, for safety she was sure, Noah didn't speak. Billie just drew comfort from his reassuring presence when he laid a gentle hand on her shoulder, then she felt something small and cold like metal being slipped into her hands. A pocket knife, she wondered, feeling its shape?

Boots crossed the floor, the door was pulled shut again and bolted with a thump. Then all was quiet. She didn't dare move for a long while until she was sure they were gone and would not return. Only then did she feel it was safe.

Fiddling to get it open without dropping it, she gingerly slipped the blade facing outward away from her skin and began slowly cutting the ropes. Damn hard when her fingers barely reached anywhere. After a while when the first tie weakened, she wriggled it free and the rope slipped from her wrists. She rubbed them for a moment then removed her blindfold.

Billie glanced around. She guessed right. Teddy Morton's old house. She was in a living area with a fireplace, rubbish and cobwebs everywhere. Left abandoned to slowly crumble into ruin.

She sat a moment because her head was pounding eventually pushed herself to stand. She teetered and grabbed the chair to steady herself, feeling light-headed and sick. Taking deep breaths, she shuffled toward the door. When she turned the knob and pushed, it didn't give. Then remembered it being locked from the outside.

Heaving a sigh at her confusion, Billie turned and walked carefully through the cottage to the kitchen with its cast iron stove still in place. Torn lace curtains hung in ragged strips from the windows. She tried the back door and, after a decent shove, it opened.

The glare of daylight and the cold chill hit her with bracing force. Billie gulped in a deep breath and moaned against the pain in her head.

What she wouldn't give right now for a glass of water and painkillers.

If the police were out looking for Noah and the other guy, Manny, she didn't want to head out into the open without checking the situation first. After being knocked out and kidnapped, she didn't want to stop a stray bullet. Scanning the paddocks around and the sky, Billie couldn't see any sign of them.

Using a veranda post for support, she stepped onto the ground and stumbled halfway around the house to the front door. The track in from the road led off to her left. Only thing for it was to just start walking. Slowly. And hope she was found soon.

She staggered the full length of the farm track and through the bushland back to the narrow sealed local road. Hoping her memory served her right, she headed north in what she hoped was the right direction back to town.

At one point she vaguely registered a chopper buzzing somewhere overhead. At a bridge over a creek, she stopped to scoop up a handful of icy cold running water to ease her thirst. She wasn't particularly hungry, although breakfast at the roadhouse hours ago seemed like a lifetime but she sure was in pain, groggy and exhausted. With not a single vehicle in sight yet on this quiet back road, Billie decided to sit and rest a while. Build up some energy to keep going.

Next thing Billie knew she was being shaken awake. She felt cold and the ground was hard beneath her. Opening her eyes revealed the best sight in the world. Noah's concerned face bending over her.

'Nice place for a nap.'

She moaned. 'I need drugs and a soft bed.'

Strong arms made short work of scooping her up and sliding her into the passenger seat beside him in the ute. Billie vaguely registered Buddy's soft yaps from the rear tray, hands clicking her seat belt and the rumble of an engine. He had found her. They were safe.

As they moved off, she heard him murmur, 'Sorry it took so long to come back for you. Let's get you to hospital for some medical advice on that bump and bruise.'

Billie thought a cold compress and some pain killers might be enough but she didn't have the strength to disagree and sank into a doze.

Chapter 10

Billie spent a few hours at outpatients, Noah by her side, as she underwent checks and scans, and her injury was examined. Because she had been only briefly unconscious and mostly aware of events following, although with a splitting headache, her injury was diagnosed as a mild to moderate concussion.

Finally, relaxed and pain-free after injections, she was released with a warning.

'She'll be staying with me,' Noah said.

She was?

'I'll keep an eye on her.'

He would?

Billie hardly felt able to object. As Noah drove her back to the homestead, she asked, 'So are you done with the drug bust?'

'Yep. I'm all yours.'

'Top thought.' She grinned. 'By the way, thanks for the pocket knife.'

'You're welcome.'

'How come you and Manny ended up together?'

'He was one of the ute drivers who took the drugs to isolated distribution houses in the area and the only one to escape when the police raided the jetty and the Lowe property. While Manny was on the run, there was a risk he would contact the top boss and let him know what had gone down. He was on foot and we didn't know if he had a mobile. The investigation squad decided to keep the bust quiet.'

'That's why there was nothing on the news.'

'If the boss guy lived in Australia, there was less chance of him getting away overseas until he was captured. I offered to track Manny and was about to pounce at the farm but he'd knocked you out by the time I got to him. So I had to play along, which at least meant I could keep an eye on you.'

'What happened when you left Teddy's house? Once I was free I didn't see you anywhere.'

'I overpowered and disarmed him.'

'You must be good. That was taking a risk.'

'The police team had eyes on me at all times. If anything went wrong, they could pull me out.'

'Were you bugged?' she asked as they turned off the main road and through the farm gate.

'Microchip tracker implant.'

Billie's interest sharpened at that disclosure. 'For real? How does that work?'

Noah gave a soft smile and chuckled as they pulled up outside the homestead. Her SUV parked exactly where she had left it in the front yard much earlier. He seemed in no hurry to leave the ute.

'Simple medical procedure. They insert it just under the skin so nothing is visible if the criminals suspected me and did a body search. It was done before this whole operation started because my movements were unpredictable.'

'So it's still on you now?'

Noah shrugged. 'It will be removed soon. Police will arrange it when the dust settles. This was a huge op. You wouldn't believe the scale of it. Depending on what the police learn from who squeals the loudest, it's likely there are overseas connections.'

Billie yawned. 'I'm so glad it was a success and you're safe.'

Noah caught her sign of exhaustion, amused. 'Let's get you some food and rest.'

'Sorry,' she groaned. 'You've had a harder day than me.'

'You've had a hit on the head.'

They moved indoors and while Billie huddled in a chair wrapped in a blanket, Noah did his thing. Fired up the old stove, filled the kettle and set it boiling then opened a can of soup and heated it up for her.

As she made a poor effort to eat, he said, 'I lit an open fire in my room. You can use my mattress.'

'Where will you sleep?'

'I've can snooze anywhere. I'll roll out my kit on the floor close by.'

When she finished her meagre attempt at trying to find an appetite, Noah helped her into his room. Although tired, when she settled down with two pillows and a thick doona, Billie discovered she couldn't sleep.

'Need more painkillers?' Noah frowned in concern, sitting on his sleeping bag, arms around his knees.

She shook her head. 'What happened to young Mason and his girlfriend?'

'Made it to the airport but didn't get to use their first class ticket or any of the drug money because they'll freeze his bank accounts.'

'Where was he planning to go?'

'I hear South America is attractive for criminals. Or he could have disappeared in any large city of the world, changed his looks and kept a low profile. A country where you can speak the language and blend in, providing you have enough money for your new life. Plenty of countries have no extradition treaty, lots of government corruption and won't look for you unless you cause trouble. But it might mean paying people off to stay hidden.' Noah's gaze covered her with affection yet also a hint of caution. 'Sure you can't sleep?'

It was now or never. She sat up a little. 'Not until I apologise I guess. For staying here when I shouldn't. Trying to find you when I should have waited. Causing you trouble. None of today would have happened if I'd done as you suggested in the first place.'

He regarded her steadily for a while before saying softly, 'Why didn't you? What's your excuse?'

Billie's throat choked up with so many unshed tears but she pushed them back and managed to say, 'Because I was worried-'

'You didn't think I could handle myself?'

'Of course not. I just-' Damn it but she couldn't form the words.

'What?' he prompted.

He was enjoying this. 'Because I hadn't heard from you.'

'Billie. I told you, I'd be in touch. If you'd waited a few more hours I would have contacted you.'

'I know that now.'

'Would have saved us both a lot of trouble.'

'True.' What else could she say? Noah was right. She'd flown with her emotions and made the wrong choice. Big mistake. That impatience thing again.

Noah rose from his sleeping bag and moved past her to stoke the fire and add more wood. 'You should have stayed put,' he said softly, crouching down beside her.

'Holly's words exactly,' she groaned. At his curious expression, she added, 'From the Coach Roadhouse.'

'Ah, that Holly.' He hesitated and she watched his mind connect. 'That where you were staying?'

'Yeah. Damn!' Billie put a hand up to her foggy head. 'I just remembered. When I left this morning, I promised to let her know I was okay. She'll be frantic. Can I use your phone? Mine's still in the car and probably needs charging by now.'

'Sure.' Noah handed over his mobile. 'Do you have the number?'

'Yeah. On my phone,' she pulled a face. 'Which is in my car.'

Noah grinned and rose. 'I'll go get it.'

While he was absent, Billie put both hands to her head and wondered how she could have done so many dumb things in a single day. She had always considered herself intelligent. Switched on. Thinking ahead, planning, making sure all her ducks were in a row. Her professional work demanded it.

When Noah returned and handed it over, the device still held a small percentage, enough so she could check her contact list and type the number into Noah's phone.

Billie deliberately kept the conversation short. She was okay, had found Noah, would give details tomorrow. She hung up and handed back Noah's phone. He took hers and plugged it into a charger.

Returning, he sat beside her mattress on the floor. 'You were safe at the roadhouse. Why did you leave?'

Good question. She simply wasn't sure she could give him an honest answer.

'I know you said you were worried and hadn't heard but, deep down, you have to admit knowing I would keep my word and be in touch.' When she stalled, he pressed, 'Billie?'

Sitting right next to her, Noah was too close and not close enough. 'I don't know.' She grew frustrated, felt cornered into confessing new feelings that had surfaced for this man in recent weeks which were hard to voice. Finally admitted, 'I guess I did.'

'Sure there's not some other reason?'

'Should there be?'

Noah let out a deep laugh and the sound melted her insides, even made her momentarily forget her physical misery and the emotional upheaval this man caused. To have grown such a strong attraction and longing for him seemed incredible when she had been so recently bumped out of what she thought was a meaningful genuine relationship.

She sensed his gaze on her, waiting for a response. And he was leaning closer, one strong arm on the mattress beside her. Talk about a rock and a hard place.

When she mustered the courage, Billie said simply, 'Melbourne was too far. I found I wanted to be closer. I thought if I stuck around, when I heard from you…'

Noah raised his free hand and stroked the side of her face. 'There'd be a chance we'd see each other again?'

She was drowning in those blue eyes. 'I guess.'

'You over David?'

'Who?' she whispered, teasing.

'You sure?'

'Just kiss me again, okay.'

She probably shouldn't have asked because Noah's lips and touch did amazing things, igniting a passion greater than with any other man. When his hand slid up into her thick hair and he pulled her close, the depth and need behind his kisses equalled her own, filling her with a sense of wholeness she'd never felt before.

Wonderful yet scary stuff, when only weeks before she had been engaged to another and about to commit her life to him.

This explosion of excitement with Noah felt so right yet also concerned her that, because it was happening so suddenly after David, they were rushing headlong into something that might not survive or she might regret. Right at this heavenly moment, that last possibility was beyond her imagination.

She decided not to dwell on negatives. They were both adults. This wasn't their first experience. One day at a time and taking it steady would soon reveal whether this electric attraction between them was meant to be.

Noah finally drew away. 'Best we leave it there,' he murmured. 'You need rest.'

Warmed and relaxed, comforted by his returned feelings, Billie couldn't disagree. 'I believe I'll sleep soundly now.'

He gave that sexy low chuckle again which always pleasantly affected her insides. Moved, she didn't resist stealing another kiss before she settled under the doona, weary but content.

After a surprisingly sound sleep, next morning Billie woke feeling little pain and much clearer in the head. Noah was nowhere to be seen, his sleeping bag already neatly rolled up but she could smell the aroma of breakfast underway.

Taking it steady, she wandered down the hallway. Noah had his back to her, cooking at the wood stove, Buddy at his side. The dog noticed her first. He trotted over and nuzzled her.

Noah turned. 'Morning. How's the patient?'

'Better.' After living in the lake shack for two weeks and aware of water restrictions on dwellings in the country, she asked, 'Do you have enough water for a bath?'

He nodded. 'Sure. Bathroom's just behind you on the right.'

'Thanks.'

Billie remembered the old claw foot bath from her first brief tour before Noah had even finished all the flooring. She dropped in the plug and turned on the squeaky taps, undressing while it filled. Sinking into the water, she closed her eyes with contentment. Apart from a pile of towels, a bar of soap and a sponge, the basic room was bare. Floorboards had been beautifully sanded but not stained. Noah was certainly putting a lot of labour and time into this restoration.

Lingering for a while, amused that if she sat up a bit she could peep over the half window sill to the homestead yard and paddocks beyond, Billie contemplated all that she must do now to get cracking on her future. A daunting prospect.

She needed to stick around for a few days because she had personal, business and family matters to consider and finalise before returning to the city to reshuffle her life. So many decisions to be made, considerations still up in the air to juggle around. So many unknowns yet to become clear.

But first she needed to force herself from this luxurious tub, get dressed and eat, realising her appetite had returned and she looked forward to breakfast.

Out in the kitchen, running fingers through her damp hair, she found Buddy eating from his food bowls by the fire and Noah with an almost empty plate in front of him at the table.

He rose. 'Hungry?'

She nodded. 'Surprisingly.'

'Good sign.'

Moments later, Noah placed freshly scrambled eggs, tomato and toast triangles in front of her. 'Thank you. This looks delicious.'

As she began to eat, Noah asked, 'So what are you plans now? Going back to the shack or heading home?'

'Neither actually. To be honest, I'd feel awkward returning to the lake. I don't want to impose on the Lowe family and all they must be going through right now. Not to mention social media scrutiny on such a high profile family. At some point, I'm going to have to approach Sasha which promises to be a difficult conversation but we've been friends since school. I'm sure our friendship will survive.'

'Sure. Don't mean to complicate things for you but you're welcome to stay here at the farm. I could set up another room for you. No strings,' he murmured, holding her gaze. 'Give you time to think through everything. Now the police operation is done, I'll be working around the farm and on this house. Happy to be a sounding board if you need to talk.'

'That's a really generous offer, Noah.' She paused and confessed honestly, 'You might be more of a distraction than I need right now.'

'I believe we'd kick along okay. I really enjoy your company. Plenty of tracks and paddocks to get away on your own. Come and go as you please. Motor bike's at your disposal and Buddy loves long walks.' His shoulders lifted into an easy shrug that was becoming endearing and familiar. 'If you're here, you're here. If you're not, you're not.'

'Tempting. I'll think about it. I should get out to the roadhouse. Collect my belongings. Depending on where I stay. Chat to Holly and Gracie. Maybe they can help me decide,' Billie said wryly.

"Not sure you should be driving yet. It's not even 24 hours since the blow to your head.'

'I feel much better this morning. Promise I'll take it easy. Plus it's way past time I paid a visit to my mother. Not sure how I'll be received. I've been a negligent daughter. My fault. Prejudice against Jack and using that as an excuse to rarely come up for a visit.'

'Hope it goes well for you.' He kissed her with gentle affection before she left.

Billie glanced at the brick home sitting empty on her way out of the farm. It would make a great rental if Noah wasn't planning on ever living there again. So many decisions still to make in his life, too.

At the roadhouse, Holly beamed across the counter as Billie walked in. 'You're back!'

'Not sure I'm staying. When would you and Gracie be free for a chat?'

'She's in her office.' Holly scanned the unusually quiet restaurant. 'And I could manage a break for ten minutes. The girls will cover for me. Everything okay?'

'Need some female advice. Another opinion would be helpful.'

'Okay. Go grab a seat while I make your usual soy cappuccino then I'll go see how Gracie is situated.'

Billie's coffee arrived within minutes and she sipped it slowly waiting for Holly to return.

When the waitress re-appeared it was with a thumbs up and a smile. 'Bring your drink and follow me.'

As always, Gracie was her usual honest and welcoming self, giving Billie a quick tight hug. 'Good to see you back safe considering I thought you made the wrong decision.'

'Holly said you weren't happy and I had reservations myself.'

'Well you're here now. What's up my dear?' She indicated they should all take up places on the sofas and chairs to one side of her office. Holly sat beside Billie and Gracie settled opposite.

'I won't bore you with details but, bottom line, my family is broken. Alcoholic father and fragile mother.'

Gracie moaned softly and leant forward, resting a hand on Billie's knee, but she didn't speak. The gesture was almost Billie's undoing.

Here Gracie and Holly were interacting like mother and daughter, and they weren't even related. A bond created through circumstances of life throwing them together. More than anything in the world, Billie longed to have such a relationship with Heather.

Pushing aside her emotions, Billie pushed on. 'Three brothers and three sisters. Only some of us had the courage and drive to leave and make a life elsewhere. Not being critical. Some people are simply content to let life lead them along and not have any particular direction.

'Point is, in the past I chose to distance myself from my parents when it was really my father that I didn't want to ever see again. I rarely return to visit and only briefly see my mother when I do. Might only make a token effort to meet two of my sisters but there's no connection and we don't have much in common. They both have partners and kids. Neither of them is married. Again, not a judgement. Just letting you know the family situation. My oldest brother is a thug like our father so I never see him. If I do, I'm polite but ignore him. I've heard him refer to me as the *ice bitch*.'

'Plenty of personalities in your family then,' Gracie said tactfully.

Holly simply said, 'I was an only child.'

'What specifically do you want from us?' Gracie asked.

One of the hardest questions she was obliged to try and answer in years. Billie held back tears. This was cutting deep to the root of what she wanted to achieve.

'I guess your opinion and blessing to go see my mother and beg her to leave my father so she can at least live the rest of her life in peace. But I understand I have no right to force her. The decision must be voluntary.'

'If she refuses?' From Gracie.

'It will break my heart. I've reflected on many things this past month. Lots of changes I want to make to my own life but also try and improve my mother's position. But it's going to create havoc in the family. My brother and father will rage because they won't have a punching bag and housekeeper anymore. Not sure what my sisters here will think.

'My youngest sister, Meredith, in Melbourne thinks I should just leave them all be. She's not heartless, comes home every few weeks when her busy work schedule allows, makes sure Mum is still alive then leaves. She's our legal member of the family and knows what our mother could do if she would just agree to help herself. But it's entirely up to Heather and she's not a strong person.'

'If you really want to raise the subject, do so, but tread very carefully. Just hint. Don't push.' This wise and crisp advice from Gracie.

When Billie glanced at Holly, the girl shrugged. 'You know my situation. In your shoes, I would also make sure your mother knows how much you love her. We never know when we're going to lose the ones we love.' The girl was obviously referring to her own mother's sudden disappearance and the lost years they would never share. 'And let her know she has your full support whatever she decides. Does she have your mobile number?'

Billie nodded. 'Always has but she's never used it and there must have been so many times over the years when she needed help.'

'I'll bet you already know in here,' Gracie rested a hand on her heart, 'what you want to do.'

'You're right. I do. Guess I just needed reassurance. Not like me, actually. Had a few curve balls thrown at me recently, relationships and friendships coming out of nowhere, good and bad.' She glanced at Holly and smiled.

Billie then raised her attraction with Noah. 'He's offered me a room in the old homestead he's renovating while I sort out a few things.'

'Well, my dear, that decision will come from the romantic place in your heart.'

'Holly?' Billie asked.

Her friend looked uncomfortable. 'You're asking the wrong person. I've never had a serious boyfriend. But I guess if I knew him to be an honest good man, I'd risk it.'

'That's my issue really. Not so much a problem because I've only known Noah for weeks and we had this instant attraction thing flare up. Two months ago I was engaged. It's kind of thrown me off balance in every way.'

'The whole district knows the Sutton family,' Gracie said. 'They've been a solid part of the farming community here for generations. Grandparents and parents. Noah is admired here even in the short time since his return. Has the cutest little girl. Brings her in here for ice cream every time she visits.' She frowned, shaking her head. 'Tragic about his brother.'

Holly glanced at her employer. 'We'd love you to stay here but being with Noah might make more sense. Closer to town and your family, less travelling.'

Billie finished her coffee and rose. 'Guess I was leaning that way, too.' She hugged the women warmly. 'Thanks, girls.'

'Don't be a stranger,' Gracie insisted.

'Keep in touch,' Holly said.

'Promise.'

After she packed up her belongings in the roadhouse cabin and piled her suitcase into the SUV, Billie played a hunch. Before she went to see her mother, she made a phone call and arranged a late afternoon appointment.

Chapter 11

Billie pulled up outside her parents' dilapidated house and sighed. It would be the worst dwelling on any street. With all the growth after winter rains, the grass hadn't been mowed recently. Weatherboards needed a coat of paint and another of Johnny's car wrecks sat proudly in the front yard. She prayed her oldest brother wasn't home. Maybe he was working for once.

Steeling herself for whatever she encountered inside, Billie strode up to the door and knocked loudly. The wire screen was ajar and she could hear the sound of voices or the television.

As the door squeaked open, Billie held her breath and tensed.

'Sibilla.' Heather Gibbs didn't hide her surprise at seeing her daughter and pushed the door wider. 'I heard you were back. Was hoping for a visit.'

Despite a difficult life, her mother had weathered the tough times. There were a few more lines on her face. Her short wavy grey hair, slacks and hand knit sweater she may have made herself or bought cheaply from an op shop, showed a measure of personal pride in her appearance that hadn't been there before.

At the look of simple pleasure on her mother's face to see her oldest daughter again, Billie felt a rush of sadness and regret, and held her in a firm hug. 'I'm sorry, Mum. I needed some time alone. Is Jack around?' Billie always found difficulty in referring to him as her father.

'Goodness, no. He'll be at the pub and betting on the races.'

Billie wondered with what money? She hoped it wasn't a big slice of their pension. Before she had a chance to ask about his violence, her mother continued.

'Comes home to eat,' Heather added. 'I don't mind. Leaves me in peace these days. He's gettin' slower, on account of his hard living and anger I guess.'

Although the humble house was messy outside, as they moved through, the interior was another story. The small living area was neat and clean. Her mother had always been a thorough and tidy homemaker and seamstress. Billie wasn't really surprised to see the familiar old sewing machine set up on the kitchen table surrounded by material and a basket spilling over with tape, pins and scissors.

'I'll just put the kettle on to boil and we can have a cuppa in the front room.'

'You doing okay?' Billie asked quietly.

Heather patted her hand. 'I can earn a tidy sum every fortnight from my sewing, cash in hand,' she pointed out, 'without affecting my pension. I'm fine dear.' While the kettle sang, she laid out homemade biscuits and slices of teacake on a plate. 'I would call your sisters but they're both working. I mind the children when I can but with this order,' she waved an arm at her sewing, 'I don't have time this week so they'll be in day care.'

Billie assessed her mother. She seemed more positive now, stronger, as though she had moved beyond her previous acceptance of her life's situation, and wondered how the change had come about. When the time was right, she would ask.

'Where are the girls working?'

'Courtney's on the checkouts at the IGA, as many shifts as she can get really. She and Chris have the two boys now, Oscar and Toby. And Brittany's just started in hospitality at a local café, mainly lunch times. Ryan's such a decent man and helpful father now Isabelle's just turned one. She's a handful. I do spoil her a bit, of course, after two grandsons.' Heather removed a photograph from under a magnet on the refrigerator and handed it to her daughter. 'Took that about a month ago.'

Billie's heart melted as she brushed a finger over the image of three quite beautiful children. She was an auntie three times over and had never met her nephews and niece. There was so much in her life she needed to address and correct. Making an effort to reconnect with her family would definitely be pushed higher on the list. As Holly kept reminding her, life was short and precious, no time to waste.

'I hope I get to meet them next time. How about Johnny?'

'Still as tough as his father,' Heather said bluntly. 'Always seems to find work but rarely has a steady girlfriend. Leastways not that he brings home to meet me,' she smiled and poured two mugs of white tea. Her mother remembered and, on reflection, Billie wouldn't have expected less. 'If you grab that plate, let's go into the front room.'

As they settled on the old sofa and before they talked about anything else, Billie needed to reveal her own altered personal circumstances. 'I don't have happy news about my own life. My engagement to David is off.'

'Oh, Sibilla,' her mother frowned in genuine concern. When Billie explained the reason, Heather said firmly, 'Well in that case, he's not good enough and didn't deserve you. That why you wanted time alone?'

Billie nodded and said candidly, 'After watching Jack mistreat you, I thought I chose wisely. Turns out living together for a while lets you see the real person. If I don't have honesty and respect from a partner, I walk away.'

Heather's lip trembled and in little more than a whisper, she said, 'All my life, I accepted what was dealt to me.' She gave Billie a meaningful glance.

Billie reached out and took her mother's hand. 'I know. I want to thank you for everything you did for all of us kids under impossible circumstances.'

'I appreciate that since you didn't have the best role models. But that was in the past. I've made changes.'

'You do seem happier. Can I ask why?'

'Your father never respected me but, some months ago,' she hesitated, her expression clouded, in memory, Billie believed, 'he went too far. Jack hurt me bad and I'd had enough. As it happened, Courtney arrived and called an ambulance. Hospital examinations and questions meant reporting it and the police became involved. He was charged and released and we're both still living under the same roof but your father knows I'm moving out soon as I can. Getting a divorce. I've spoken to Meredith already.'

Billie filled with hope for her mother. Heather had finally gained the courage to make change happen. Ironic they should both be in transition to the next stage of their lives. 'Let me know how I can help in even the smallest way.'

'If it came to that, one of the girls would take me in so I have a backup if I need it. And

Johnny's on notice. Time he got responsible. I've given him till end of year to find another place. After Christmas, he's out. To be honest, I don't want him around anymore. I'm getting too weary. Besides,' she chuckled, 'I'd get more pension being a single person.'

After such a reassuring and uplifting visit, Billie's mind was set to rest. 'I'd love to take you out for coffee or lunch while I'm still here?'

'Well that would be a treat.'

'Don't suppose you have a mobile?'

Heather scoffed. 'The girls bought me one cheap with a basic plan. Keep it on top of the fridge.' She disappeared to fetch it.

As Billie keyed the number into her own phone, she wondered how all of her mother's recent trauma could have escaped her. Crushing truth? She had been too busy and caught up in her own city life to spare a moment for this woman who she owed so much. She could never make up for the past but damn sure she would be there for her in the future.

Edging toward another subject she had been longing to raise, Billie asked, 'Did you see in the news about the local drug bust?'

'Yes. On the Lowe place. Their boy was involved. The police did a great job of getting that stuff off the street.'

'Noah Sutton was involved in helping the investigation.'

'Margaret and Bill's youngest?'

Billie nodded. 'He was in the Air Force but he's retired from service and returned home to the farm. He went undercover flying the plane in and out of the lake.'

'Sounds like a brave man.'

'He is. I've gotten to know him recently.' Billie paused to take a deep breath, hoping her mother didn't think she was crazy so soon after breaking off with David. 'He's become special to me, Mum. Wish me better luck next time, huh?' She tried to restrain tears of joy to see her mother's warm understanding smile.

After a moment of contemplation, Heather said quietly, 'You know, I don't hold with that old saying, *Things come to those who wait.* Think how much time we waste. Bugger that.' Billie's surprised gaze turned to her mother and they both burst out laughing together. 'Once we can knock aside our fears, I'm a new believer in grabbing what you need to be in a better place. Keep that in mind with Noah.'

Wise words, Billie knew, and a subtle hint nudging her in a definite direction. She checked the time on her phone. 'I have an appointment soon.' They rose and she hugged her mother, amused and moved by Heather's new strength and positive attitude. 'I'll be in touch.'

Driving away from the Gibbs house, Billie felt such a sense of relief and pride for her mother. As well as personal promise on her own account from the significant meeting she was about to hold.

After positive discussions, Billie walked from the office in town on a high. With her mother's circumstances on the way to being sorted out and her own career possibilities looking firm, she grabbed a bag of fresh fruit and a cooked chicken from the local market before driving back out to the farm.

With no immediate sign of Noah, Billie dumped her food bags on the kitchen table. She had only been gone a day but smelt paint. Following her nose, she discovered he had stained the bathroom floor. Looked amazing, highlighted every colour in the timber making it glossy and fresh. Noah Sutton sure was a handyman with taste. Well, she grinned, he liked me, didn't he?

Billie headed outside and found him striding toward her with Buddy at his side. He must have seen her arrive. She thrilled at the sight of him, muscled legs in denims and his favourite thick checked shirt only half buttoned, sleeves rolled up and a black tee underneath. He was a vision to behold and no mistake.

When he reached her, he didn't muck about. Hauled her close with one big arm at her waist and dragged her hard up against him while she was thoroughly kissed. And missed?

'You look happy.'

'I am. Went to visit my mother and she's doing great. She'll be leaving Jack as soon as she can find a place to live.' Billie related the details of Heather's transformed situation.

'That took guts.' He cast her an uncertain glance. 'Wasn't sure I'd see you again.'

A big physically magnificent man like Noah Sutton standing close and looking so vulnerable melted Billie's heart with amusement. 'Doesn't sound like your usual confidence,' she teased, waited a heartbeat then asked, 'Your offer still on the table?'

'Damn straight,' he drawled beaming. 'Let's go inside and get you settled.' Hand in hand, he walked Billie into the homestead, Buddy at their heels. 'The front room is the biggest. I've just stained the floorboards in the bathroom so you can't take a bath or shower until morning.'

'I noticed. Good job!'

As they entered the chosen front room with its matching panoramic double sash windows the same as the sitting room opposite across the hallway, Billie stopped. 'You've already set it up! I thought you weren't expecting me.'

A lazy knowing grin edged that gorgeous mouth. 'A man always lives in hope.'

'All your dreams coming true, huh?' Noting the two mattresses on the floor, she asked, 'You fixing to join me?'

Leaning against the door frame, he sent her a steamy gaze. 'If I did that, we'd only need the one.' He let her reflect on that for a bit, but their shared gaze revealed they were both on the same page with the direction of his thinking. 'It's for Rosie. She's coming at the weekend,' he explained. 'Hope you don't mind but you'll have to share. Can you stay that long?'

'Don't mind at all and, yes, I can. You really want me here?'

Noah pushed himself away from the door and sauntered into the room toward her. 'I know its early days between us but, yeah, I'd like to introduce you to my daughter.'

Billie recalled her mother's words about grabbing what you needed. Daunting to be meeting this man's little girl, all part of the whole Noah Sutton package but she was also delighted to be asked. 'And I'd love to meet her.'

Billie had planned to leave by the weekend. Noah's invitation meant living here for five days instead of two. The new situation could be considered both a blessing and a curse. It meant meeting Rosie and getting to know her. And any extra time with Noah would always be good but it also involved dealing with this building chemistry between them.

There was only one way that was going to be released!

When they moved into the kitchen, Noah noticed her bags of food on the table. 'Smells good.'

Billie chuckled. 'Just a bought roast chicken. If I can get the hang of that stove,' she glanced at the black monster that Noah had no problem taming, 'I can do some vegetables.'

'You're a guest. I'll cook. But you could go check the chooks are all in the yard and close their door for the night.'

Billie sidled up to him. 'How about you do that and I'll make dinner? As a thank you for having me.'

Noah raised his arms and backed away, smiling. 'Sure. We'll work out the terms later.' His teasing innuendo promised excitement between them. He added more wood to the fire and disappeared outside again.

Unlike her mother, Billie did not often feel at home in a kitchen. She rummaged in the refrigerator, found a saucepan and chopped vegetables. While they boiled, she dissected the chicken and set it on a plate. Finding it all a simple pleasure in the cosy warmth being pushed out by the old stove.

It occurred to her that this living arrangement was only temporary and she would need to leave in a few days. So, until then, instead of dwelling on how little time they would have together, she would indulge in every sense and memory to make the most of her time here with this man.

They took their time over dinner, boosting the single light globe hanging from the ceiling with a pair of fat candles on the table, flickering out a much softer glow. Noah's hair took on a golden sheen. Billie couldn't keep her eyes from him and his every movement. Aware and shocked at her intense developing feelings.

They stood side by side at the sink washing and drying the dishes. Later, it took a while for them to break apart and head for separate rooms. When Noah had finally finished touching and kissing her to distraction, Billie closed the door and leant back against it, breathing heavily. Her desire for him was growing with every loaded glance and physical contact. She knew they would both surrender when the moment was right and, to be honest, she couldn't wait much longer. They only had two days alone until Rosie arrived.

Next morning, Noah knocked on her door but didn't wait to be invited. Instead, he strolled right in before she had barely woken and rolled over. 'Kitchen cabinets are going in today so while the guys are ripping out the old and installing the new, I have a surprise for you.'

'A surprise. I don't get a hint?'

He shrugged. 'Let's live dangerously.'

Billie was thinking they were doing that simply by being in each other's company. 'Will it take long?'

'Nope. Hour or so.'

Noah had promised her free time. Walks with the dog. Time to herself. She should be

working on arrangements for when she was
back in the city next week. Oh, what the hell.
'Okay, you're on.'

Chapter 12

'Where are we going?' Billie asked as they rumbled along a gravelled road between paddocks in Noah's ute.

'You'll see.'

It was only a short trip before they turned off onto the track leading in to Reedy Lake. During her stay, Billie had only been at the opposite end in the shack on the Lowe property close to Noah's farm, so her attention sharpened as they approached from the other direction.

She soon understood why. Noah pulled up near the jetty where crime scene tape still cordoned off a large area. The float plane was still tied up at the jetty and a lone police officer looked to be on duty. Billie had an idea where this outing might be going.

When Noah eased from the ute and strode toward the officer, Billie stepped out, too.

'Noah Sutton.' The men shook hands. 'I'm the pilot helping the investigation.'

The officer brightened. 'Yeah, I heard about you.'

'This bird fuelled and ready to go?' Noah indicated the plane at the end of the jetty.

The guard nodded. 'Just waiting for instructions.'

'I guess the official order hadn't reached you yet. I'm here to take it up for a short test flight. Make sure it's mechanically sound before being impounded.' He beckoned to Billie. 'I'll have one passenger.'

'Is that normal?' the officer queried.

'Nope,' Noah admitted and added with a shrug, 'Only be thirty minutes. The lady would sure appreciate it. She was most helpful during our investigation.'

Billie hid a grin. That was stretching the truth and this flight was anything but authorised.

Incredibly, the officer grinned and nodded in understanding. 'Expect you back within the hour.'

Noah gave him a wave, grabbed her hand and they strode down the jetty. He opened the door and held her hand as she stepped onto the top of the float and climbed inside to take up a seat. Billie watched him loosen the tie down then scramble into the cockpit beside her. She discovered it a tight space but didn't mind the cosy fit.

'Seatbelt and headphones on.'

'Clearly we're not supposed to be doing this,' Billie teased.

'We just did. Relax.' He reached over and put a firm reassuring hand on her knee.

'Thought you might want to see your home country from above.'

'That's really considerate but cheeky.'

'I guess I've learned to take more risks than I should. Sometimes you need to shake life up a bit and just do something. Stop looking at me,' he drawled, 'and make the most of the view while we've got it.'

By now the plane had drifted away from the jetty. Noah started the engine and the propeller spun. He pushed the throttle forward and they taxied out into the lake.

'Why are we turning?' Billie asked.

'Always take off into the wind. Ready?'

She nodded, as thrilled to be having this experience as spending personal time with Noah. He revved up, the engine roared and they began skimming over the water. The nose tilted back, the plane accelerated and they lifted off.

Billie knew a boost of glorious exhilaration. 'This is so cool.'

'It's the rare freedom of knowing you can go anywhere there's water.'

Billie settled back into her seat and forced herself to unwind. Tried to ignore Noah's daredevil move and instead focus on the green plains landscape stretching out below them to the distant Grampians mountains and horizon. He was right. She should enjoy this moment and her companion.

It seemed to her that every outing they took together added a level of adventure or excitement to their deepening attraction for each other. She chose not to dwell on the fact she would be leaving soon and no longer a part of Noah's daily life. And where this pull of attraction would lead. Whether they both wanted to have the other in their lives. How it was all going to work out moving forward. She shouldn't plan. Just wing it. Ha! She smiled in amusement at her own joke.

As her mind wandered, so did her gaze. They flew over winter lakes, paddock squares and winding rural creeks before banking and returning over Reedy Lake, the shack at the far end which Billie had called home for a time, the Lowe property where the presence of the law was still visible and, finally, Noah's farm.

She sank into reflection about this familiar country spread out below where she had been born and raised. Her family experience was not perfect by a long shot but Noah had known deeper tragedy and grief. The loss of his brother far too young and his parents in recent years.

By comparison, Billie still had her parents and was grateful for that. Especially reconnecting with her mother and possibly her sisters. Accepting them for who they were, but knowing she could never allow Jack into her life in any way. The worst of his past anger may have eased but unless he ever acknowledged how he mistreated his wife and family, and apologised, he was destined to remain estranged.

Now, having met Noah, both this home country and her sudden burst of appeal for him were drawing her back. As unsettling as it sounded, time apart should prove the strength of their growing awareness. For Billie, that meant being utterly hooked and besotted with her farmer. Before she left, if he didn't give her some sign or show her how he felt, tell her what was real between them, then Melbourne on her own was promising to be an emotional nightmare. In such a short time, she had grown to expect his contact and company. Felt so comfortable around him.

'You've been quiet.' Noah's voice came to her through the headphones.

'Taking it all in. Just beginning to understand how much this region means to me.' She glanced at him. 'And you.'

He reached over and briefly squeezed her hand. 'Me too.'

Descending was bittersweet. The flight was far too short but they weren't even supposed to be up here. She figured the officer below would keep their confidence.

The lake waters gradually rushed to meet them until they were landing and motoring slowly toward the jetty. As they drew closer, Noah shut off the engine and let the plane float in before jumping out to tie it down again. He helped Billie out, they quickly thanked the police officer in passing and drove back to the farm.

'That was amazing. Thank you for going to the trouble but don't do it again. I don't expect you to bend the rules for me.'

'The guy at the jetty was onto us. We're good.'

Back at the homestead, the kitchen was half in, the other half still in pieces and partly covered in sheeting waiting to be installed. Against the repaired and stained timber floor, Noah had chosen the softest gum leaf green cupboards and stone coloured counters all in a rustic style which kept the room light, perfectly suiting the home's original era. For a man, Billie was impressed with his taste. Home decorating wasn't every bloke's cup of tea.

Since the carpenters were having lunch, Noah and Billie grabbed a sandwich and joined them to eat out on the veranda. Winter had turned on a calm sunny day.

After the workmen moved back inside, Noah asked, 'You free this afternoon?'

'I should be working,' Billie moaned. 'I have so much stuff to get rolling before I even go back to Melbourne.'

'Thought I could teach you how to fish.'

'I've netted some good hauls of yabbies in my time,' she grinned in defence.

'We could borrow the boat at the shack for a while.'

'Frankly, sitting still and waiting has never been a strong trait of mine. I'll probably be bored stiff but I guess I can do some work later,' she conceded, admitting to herself it was too tempting to refuse more time with him. 'Okay, I'll give it a try.'

Noah chuckled. 'Don't sound so keen.'

'You've been warned. You may regret this.'

'I'll never regret a moment of time I get to spend with you.' He leant across and kissed her, dragging Billie to her feet and following it up with another.

'This extra persuasion in case I back out?' she murmured.

'Crossed my mind.'

'Are we even going to catch anything this time of year?' Billie helped Noah load fishing gear into the boat at the shack, then relaxed while her strong-armed sailor did his stuff and rowed them out into the middle of the lake.

'Fish metabolism is slower in winter so they don't overfeed and might be less inclined to bite. Perch are winter feeding so we should get lucky. Ready to wet a line?'

'You can stick the bait on, I'll just hold the rod.'

'We might find some brown trout so I'll hook up some mudeye.' Noah rummaged around in his tackle box and once that was done, he made a good long cast out into the water.

As they sat quietly holding their rods. Billie asked, 'Why the different coloured floats?'

'Easier to spot on the water. Each fisherman can identify his own line.'

Billie persevered for what felt like hours but was, in fact, much less. Her mind emptied of everything except the slight ripples on the surface from the light wind. She watched the length of shadows and reflections change with the path of the sun slowly heading west. Noah, on the other hand, sat still and patient. She found his quiet endurance and serenity enviable. Once or twice they were teased by nibbles and bobbing floats which amounted to nothing.

'How long does this take?'

'We should give it a while longer. We've had some interest.'

'So if we don't catch anything, we head into town for fish and chips?'

Noah grinned. 'If it's big, we only need one for a feed. Toward evening, we might get a trout or two.'

True to his word and Billie's relief, just as the late afternoon winter sun disappeared behind the eucalypts edging the lake, Noah's float disappeared and his line strained.

'You're kidding!' Billie actually grew excited.

Noah slowly reeled it in, gave it time then reeled again. 'Grab the net. We're gonna need it for this one. We're not going hungry tonight, woman. He's a cracker.'

Billie shook her head in amusement at the man's delight. Fishing was clearly in his blood. 'How can you tell?'

'He's keen.' When the fish was alongside the boat and they could see its reflection, Noah said, 'Put the net in the water underneath.'

Billie leaned forward and scooped it up, flapping and wetting them both in the process.

Noah beamed. 'A beautiful big brown trout.'

He rowed back to the shack, they unloaded their gear from the boat to the ute, their catch safely in an esky and drove home as the sun settled on the horizon.

The workmen were packing up their tools as Noah and Billie pulled up out the front of the homestead in the ute.

'All in, mate. Done and dusted,' one of them said.

Noah thanked them all, shook hands with each in turn and the crew took off in a twin cab.

While half a kitchen had showed such promise at midday, the finished version was gorgeous. Billie whistled low as they reached the end of the hallway and entered the completely new space. 'You'll be able to do some serious cooking here.'

'Yeah. Rosie's gonna love it.' He seemed underwhelmed and Billie wondered why. 'Wiring will be done tomorrow,' he added, turning to her with a smile. 'But tonight we'll have a cookout.'

'Liking the sound of it.'

While Noah built a fire in a pit on the sheltered side of the homestead, Billie grabbed the makings, chopped and tossed a salad. By the time she carried the dish, plates and cutlery onto the veranda, Noah had mixed and placed his damper in a cast iron pot and nestled it into the coals. She sat in a camp chair with a glass of beer while Noah scaled and prepared their catch for a pan.

When the trout started gently sizzling, Billie loaded their plates with salad and Noah rescued the damper from the pot. After it cooled a bit, he sliced it into thick chunks. Because it all looked and smelt so delicious, Billie suddenly realised the extent of her hunger. No meal had ever tasted so good.

As they ate with only random conversation, Billie considered this life in the country which had been so distant to her only a month ago, having been eager to escape and entrenched herself in the city for years. The simplicity and peace of living out here were difficult for any urban dweller to achieve. They had to travel far or leave to find it, while it existed on her doorstep. Which gave her pause for thought about the possibility of making the country her home again one day. So much still unresolved and undecided in her world right now, her normally organised mind was confused. She let out a long sigh as she stared into the flames while Noah rose to pile more logs on the fire.

He sat beside her again, leaned closer and took her hand. 'You have a great smile.' He held up a finger of warning and stalled a grin. 'Don't show it to me now.'

'I'm sorry?'

'You're looking quite serious there.'

Once she realised he was teasing her to raise a smile, there was no way Billie could hide one. Drawing up her knees, feeling relaxed and cosy, if not fully content, she admitted, 'Just reflecting on a wonderful day and my time here. Thinking that I need to make a heap more phone calls and emails in the morning, setting up appointments for when I get back to the city. And I should phone Mum again to arrange lunch with her, too.'

'Tomorrow's sorted then?'

'For me. What are you doing?'

'Electrician will be here early so the power will be off for the morning while he rewires parts of the house. Gives me a chance to take a break from renovating and get out around my flock. Check the crops.'

Noah rose and crossed to the ute where he turned on the radio to country music and left the door open. Returning, he drew Billie up into his arms, placing one hand around her waist and holding the other for dancing.

With his cheek against her hair, he murmured, 'Lot to be said for old fashioned romance. The miracle of a chance encounter. Nothing sexier than getting to hold your partner real close.'

To Billie nothing felt more stirring than being held tight and possessively by this man, outside in the dark, lit only by low flames from their campfire and a night sky full of stars. After a while, her arms slid up around his neck, his head lowered and their lips crushed together in powerful scorching kisses, his hands roaming all over her body.

When they stopped dancing and grew hot with breathless passion, Noah growled, 'I'm taking you inside,' and swept her up into his arms.

She threw back her head and laughed, filled with hunger for him. 'I love it when a man takes control.'

'More like losing it.'

A mattress on the floor of a half renovated old homestead and moonlight streaming in the window had never been more romantic. Billie gave herself to Noah who, she discovered more than once, sure knew how to please a woman.

It took a while before their desire was satisfied. For now. Billie finally fell into a deep

and satisfied sleep with Noah's arm slung across
her waist and his warm body spooned against
her back.

Chapter 13

Billie woke to the sun pouring through Noah's bedroom window. Realising who lay beside her, she smiled and stretched. She was about to move when a strong arm landed across her body.

'You're not going anywhere,' he drawled.

Making long slow love again was worth everything they had both been through to bring them here. She felt like she would never get enough of this man.

Afterwards, Noah raised himself on an elbow, looking down at her. 'What's up?'

'Why do you ask?'

'You don't usually wear a frown. I could feel offended but I'm getting to know when there's something on your mind.'

'I was thinking about later today when Rosie arrives. I'll admit to being a little nervous. This is her home. I'm a stranger.'

'Not to me anymore,' he chuckled. 'Relax. Outside family, you're the only other person I've wanted to bring into her life.' He gently brushed the hair back from her face. 'I want you here and she's going to love you.'

'It's a big step for me.'

'So was last night,' he murmured, nibbling her ear. 'You okay?'

Billie chuckled, as much from the fact that he was tickling her where he kissed but also because of the memory their loving had created. Which also raised the crossroad they had reached since stepping beyond that turning point. 'I'm fine. You know it was what I wanted.'

'I did get that message.' He gently stroked her cheek.

'I guess I'm feeling bewildered by how quickly my feelings have changed and moved forward. Made me realise how little actually existed in my last relationship. We were never destined to make it as a couple,' she said with honest acceptance, 'because now I know what deep feelings are possible.'

'Just so you know, my feelings for you are the same, and very real. Don't wrestle with where our relationship is going. It's wherever we want it to and where it takes us. But from my perspective, I'd be simply asking to be with you and whatever we want after that.'

From the gentle sincerity in his voice and love reflected in his eyes, Billie was finally allowing herself to believe that what she had begun to share with this man was timeless and precious.

'To be honest,' he continued, 'when Manny kidnapped you and your life was on the line, it hit home how much I would lose if you weren't around. And how much you mean to me. I did tell you to leave, you know,' he teased.

'I know,' she groaned. 'I never used to be much good at taking orders. But having experienced the trauma of my life at stake, I'm learning to listen.'

Billie heaved a sigh of disappointment when Noah left her side, but indulged in the luxury of watching him get dressed before disappearing to make breakfast in the new kitchen.

When she joined him shortly after, she tiptoed up behind him as he stood at the old stove and slid her arms around his waist. He turned into her embrace. Buzzing with exhilaration, she wrapped herself around him and tilted her head up so she could be thoroughly kissed.

After breakfast before Noah left, he said, 'Don't organise dinner. We always have takeaways and ice cream on Rosie's first night back on our way into town at the Coach Roadhouse. We did it once and she begged me the next time and every time after that. So it's become kind of a treat and tradition.'

Billie recalled Holly mentioning their routine which made her feel a little down, excluded, although she knew it was something father and daughter shared alone. There would be times that would happen. Rosie would always come first for Noah.

The electrician van arrived as he drove away toward the stock paddocks to check on his Merinos and meet with his agronomist. Later, he would travel to Ballarat to meet Michelle and pick up Rosie.

Surprised to feel such a sense of loss with Noah's departure, Billie retreated to her bedroom all morning and worked between her laptop and phone while the electricians were occupied at the back of the homestead, wiring up the new kitchen.

Her first call was to her mother, arranging lunch at one of the smaller popular cafés. Billie was amused by Heather's eager anticipation of the outing and suggestion that Brittany and little Isabelle could join them.

'Of course. Look forward to it.'

As she hung up, Billie knew a moment of simple happiness to be reconnecting with her family. Proud of her mother's courage and contentment at her stage of life after all she had endured.

The rest of the morning flew by in a heavy load of organising her old job, phoning her boss and setting up an appointment to discuss her future with the company. Even as she spoke, thoughts of negotiating a new contract and continuing with her current work situation, raised a red flag of dissatisfaction. In a single month, her entire life and future had been thrown into chaos and, already, it felt strangely distant to consider returning to it.

She checked in with the landlord at her new apartment where she had lived since David's shock announcement. Billie was relieved to hear that her mail was being held as instructed. How long she would stay in the city was a mystery. Initially, returning home had always been on the understanding of a brief stay out here getting her head together and returning to Melbourne.

Until a handsome local farmer had clomped across the deck of the shack, entered her world and stirred her emotions. Getting to know him, spend time with him, growing to depend on him had all seemed like the most natural thing to happen.

It seemed ridiculous now that she and Noah had committed themselves to each other in the closest way, not to somehow manage to physically continue to meet. Would Noah come to the city or would she commute back home here to the Wimmera? The latter would also create an ideal opportunity to keep in touch with her mother and sisters and their families, too.

Closing her laptop and dressing for lunch, Billie decided to take Noah's advice and just let life take its course. Although after last night and more to come, she hoped that journey would be driven by their need for each other.

Around midday, Billie sped into town. Her mother and Brittany, with the cutest toddler in pink swinging her short legs in a high chair, were already sitting at their booked table.

Billie greeted Heather first with a quick hug, then turned to Brittany, one of her two younger sisters remaining in town whom she had rarely seen for years since leaving at eighteen for university and the city.

As Brittany rose, Billie's first impression was astonishment. Gone was the rebellious teenager of almost a decade before with the heavy black eye makeup, red lips and tight clothes. Time had matured them all and been gracious to this sister in washed denim, a cropped matching jacket, tee shirt beneath and a scarf tossed around her shoulders. The softest wave of light perfume drifted around them as the sisters hugged.

Brittany pulled back and shook her head. 'As classy as always, Billie. Courtney and I are so proud of you and Melanie. You two got the brains for sure.'

Billie kept a hand on her arm. 'You've grown into a lovely woman yourself, Britt. Motherhood suits you.'

When they resumed their seats, Brittany beamed down at her daughter, drooling and chewing on a spoon. 'This is our little Isabelle. Teething,' she laughed.

Billie took the time to gaze a while on her niece, looking so cute and adorable in pink leggings and a warm dress, all topped by a head of curls.

'Hey sweetie.' When Isabelle smiled back at her, she felt an unaccountable rush of love for the child.

'You should see Courtney's two boys. Talk about livewires. Exact opposite of Isabelle. So glad I had a girl. I wanted a bunch of kids like Mum but after one, boy, they're expensive. My partner, Ryan, is the best.' She glanced across at Billie. 'When I was young, I know I put myself out there but I had pretty high expectations. I waited a long time to find a man who would respect me.'

Their mother reached across and patted Brittany's hand. 'He was certainly worth the wait, dear.'

'Now I've found him I'm never letting go. Hope you don't mind, Billie, but mum told me your engagement's off,' Brittany said straight up. 'Sorry, but if they don't measure up, honestly you're better off without them. I mean, look at our father. No example. Gives all men a bad name. He's a pig and Mum's well shot of him.'

As direct as always. Billie didn't miss her mother's scowl of disapproval. Sad thing was, as cruel as it sounded, her sister only spoke the truth.

'That's why I came back to the country for a while,' Billie admitted. 'Do some thinking. How to get my life sorted and move on.'

'Did it help?'

Billie glanced across at her mother who met her gaze before she turned back to Brittany. 'You'd know Noah Sutton?'

'Mr. Gorgeous Pilot? For sure. When his ute rolls into town, every single female around sits up and takes notice. Apparently keeps to himself though. Why?'

'He's become a good friend and neighbour since I was staying at the shack.'

'No way! You and him?' Billie nodded. 'That happened quick. You just ditched the other guy.'

'Actually he ditched me for another woman but that feels like so much history now. Incredible how a matter of weeks can turn your life around.'

They ordered lunch and once their meals arrived, settled to eating. From time to time, Brittany handed Isabelle a warm chip to nibble on in between lots of wonderful idle chatter. Billie had never enjoyed a girl catch up more. Reminded of all the long business lunches she had with her city girlfriends, the fancy salads and endless glasses of wine.

This here today, sitting around the table, was real. With family. Her mother, sister and niece. The kind of real she intended to focus on in her life now. Perhaps a sign, too, of closing in on thirty. For Billie, at least, the social scene had grown jaded.

Over coffee, Brittany drew a sleepy Isabelle onto her lap. 'This little miss had early lunch and it's her nap time. Mum, we should leave soon.'

Before they parted, Billie said, 'Noah has a daughter, Rosie, from his marriage. She's coming home with him this evening to stay. I've never had much to do with children. I'm more anxious than I thought I would be.'

As she bundled up Isabelle and big carryall bags, Brittany waved a hand and said, 'Be yourself. Kids are smart. They can sense a fake.'

'They're just small adults,' their mother intervened, having remained quiet for much of the meal, 'and never underestimate their intelligence. Listen to them and give them plenty of love and hugs.'

After swapping phone numbers and promises to catch up again soon, they parted. Although Billie had no idea how they would manage it, she intended to make sure it happened.

On the way home, inspired by the advice her mother and sister had shared, Billie reflected back when she was a girl and the kinds of things she and her sisters had never known but would have loved. She stopped to collect what she hoped would be a treat for Rosie, crossing her fingers the child loved what she had planned. Good thing the electrician came today.

Around mid-afternoon when she returned to the homestead, Billie spent time in the room she would share with Rosie organising the treat for her.

Billie was still concerned that she and Noah would have little time alone together while his daughter was staying and before she left in a few days. Getting her head around where this change was taking them. The most she could do right now was simply keep loving him. There was never a moment when he wasn't in her thoughts so that would have to be enough.

Anxious to hear his voice for reassurance, she phoned him.

'How's my other favourite girl?' he greeted her.

A small voice piped up, 'Daddy, who's that?'

'As you can hear, I've collected Rosie and we're on our way home. We'll have an early dinner at the roadhouse and be there around dark.'

'Great.' Feeling restless and needing headspace, she asked, 'Okay if I borrow the motorbike?'

'Sure.'

'Maybe go and check out your old farmhouse?'

There was an element of uncertainty in his tone. 'It's always unlocked.'

Billie wondered if that was wise or if, because of his apparent emotional disinterest, he simply didn't care. 'Thanks. I'll see you both later.'

When she wheeled the motorbike out of the machinery shed and legged it over ready to kick-start, Buddy suddenly appeared and leapt up behind. 'Hey, boy. You go wherever the bike goes, huh?'

To blow away the cobwebs and troubled thoughts of Rosie's imminent visit and leaving the Wimmera, Billie rode out around the homestead block perimeter, along paddock fence lines, following tracks and letting the brisk winter wind blow back her hair. Constantly checking to make sure Buddy was still on board.

Eventually, she pulled up out front of the empty Sutton farmhouse where Adam and Noah had grown up. Parking the bike, Buddy leapt off and disappeared while she stepped across the high grass toward the back door.

She turned the knob and let herself in, standing still a moment, taking in the eerie neglect, although all was otherwise neat. Dining table and chairs, lounge room furniture looking sad but all still in good condition. Could do with a clean and upgrade for sure. Which set Billie wondering yet again why Noah chose not to return here.

Could do with a repaint, new blinds or curtains and floor coverings. The basics really.

Dusty family photos stood on a sideboard and hung along the passage walls. Indoors was smaller than it appeared from outside and the garden overgrown but was all easily improved.

She wondered if she should raise the question of what Noah planned to do with this property. None of her business really but seemed such a waste of a lovely house. Definitely the elephant in the room here. On the other hand there was probably a perfectly fine explanation.

He seemed so dedicated and attached to his grandparents' old homestead, pouring so much time, work and love into it. He had his hands full with renovating the house and running the farm.

Reflecting on her own current situation, Billie knew she was falling in love with Noah. Gripped by a big and strong attraction now, much larger than any she had known before, she worried this new relationship would wither and fail. Could it withstand the distance between city and country? The challenges life would undoubtedly throw in front of them over the years? Children?

She rubbed her arms and cast a glance around her. Being logical, if she and Noah made a permanent commitment to each other, she would willingly make the sacrifice to live here. Perhaps not here in this house but his grandparents' homestead which clearly owned his affection. Could she make the country her life now when a decade before she couldn't wait to see the Wimmera landscape behind her in the bus? To ease her mind, this was a conversation she needed to initiate with Noah before she left on Monday.

When she emerged outdoors again, the electrician van drove up and stopped. The tradie wound down his window and rested an arm on it. 'All done. Connected up your bedroom too. Looks amazing,' he grinned.

'Thanks.' Billie waved, stoked to hear it. Should be a winner with Rosie, then.

She whistled for Buddy who raced around a corner of the house and joined her on the bike for the return ride back to the homestead. Inside, she discovered all new electrical points throughout and period light fittings. Noah's love and pride in this house was certainly obvious.

Billie made herself a sandwich and strolled the rooms, discovering new pictures on the walls and two family photos on a newly placed hall table. He must have done it all before he left to collect Rosie. The child would be excited to see the changes. She only hoped she equally loved the surprise in store in their shared bedroom.

It was almost dark when Billie noticed headlights coming in along the farm track off the main road and Noah's ute pulled up out front. With a level of apprehension, Billie went out onto the front veranda to meet them.

Buddy appeared from nowhere and raced straight for the ute, leaping all over Noah as he stepped out, before dashing around to the other side.

'Buddy, down.' She heard a joyful child's laughter. 'Daddy, he's happy to see me, too.'

With his gaze settled on Billie, he called out, 'Come here and meet the visitor I told you about.'

A whirlwind of small legs and flying hair ran around the front of the vehicle and grabbed her father's hand, staring up at Billie. She caught her breath. Those blue eyes and long blonde hair. Talk about a tiny mirror image of her father. Together, man and child walked up the steps.

Her heart lifted when Noah leant in for a kiss and murmured, 'How was your day?'

'Rewarding, actually.'

He hesitated. 'Get over to the other house?'

'Yeah. Still has good bones.'

With no further comment from him on that subject, he glanced down. 'Rosie, this is my friend, Billie.'

'Hello. We just had burgers and chips.'

'Nice to meet you, Rosie. And I bet you had ice cream, too, because I can see some still around your mouth.'

Rosie grinned. 'I told Daddy it was okay if you sleep in my room.'

'Well thank you. I appreciate you sharing. Actually, I have a surprise in there for you.'

Wide-eyed, the child released her father's hand and dashed indoors, Buddy whipping around them all and sneaking in behind. As Billie and Noah followed and moved inside, they hard a squeal of delight.

'Daddy, come see.'

Standing in the bedroom doorway, they watched Rosie jumping on her floor mattress like a trampoline, smiling up at the strings of fairy lights strung around the room. 'It's like a party.'

With the lights off, even though she had done it herself, Billie had to admit the glow looked amazing. 'Going well, so far,' she murmured.

Without a word, she felt Noah's arm slide around her waist and he pressed a kiss to her forehead. 'When you're done,' he said to Rosie, 'come down to the kitchen. One hot chocolate with marshmallows then bed, okay?'

While Noah disappeared, Billie lingered to watch his daughter but even a tiny tornado could get tired and she soon bounced off the mattress.

'You coming?' Rosie asked.

Billie warmed to feel included and they walked down the hall together. Halfway down, as they passed the side table, Rosie paused at the photographs. 'That's my Uncle Adam,' she looked up at Billie in case she didn't know. 'He had a really bad accident and died,' she said earnestly, 'but he's with us every day.'

Billie was touched at the sentiments clearly shared and passed on from Noah, and found it hard not to stop tears pooling in her eyes. 'I'm sure that's a comfort to your Daddy.'

A wide eyed Rosie nodded madly and her serious expression turned into a smile. 'He says good morning to him every single day. And that's my Granny Maggie and Grandpa, Bill,' she pointed to the wedding photo alongside, 'but they died already, too.'

'They were good folks.'

Rosie tilted up her head and her tiny nose wrinkled. 'You knew them?'

Billie nodded. 'A long time ago.'

'Daddy talks about them sometimes. He said it's important to remember our 'cestors.'

Amused by her pronunciation, Billie smiled, 'It certainly is.'

'We go and talk to them in the cemetery. I know where they're sleeping,' she said excitedly. As quick as a flash, Rosie's attention was diverted when she burst into the new kitchen. 'It's like a real house now, Daddy.'

By now, Billie was beyond relaxed, filled with contentment that Noah was home again and the sense of calm his presence always brought. Rosie was a chatty bundle of energy and happiness, openly trusting and accepting of the people in her father's life.

The child had barely finished her warm drink before she yawned. Noah quietly scooped her up, Rosie's arms instinctively wrapping around his neck. Billie melted at the sight. If today's experience with little Isabelle and now Rosie, was any indication, it was clear that children swiftly embedded themselves into your heart.

She waited in the front sitting room, hearing low voices from the next door bedroom, until Noah came to find her. 'Never a problem getting her to sleep.' He settled on the sofa beside her.

'Rosie's very perceptive and she's right, you know. This lovely old building is becoming what it was meant to be again. A family home. All credit to you.'

'I'm enjoying it. Something I felt I wanted to do.'

'What plans for your weekend with Rosie?'

'Hope you're expecting to be a part of it, too.'

'I'd love it. Rosie's a sweetie.' She paused. 'I met my niece Isabelle today. She's just recently turned one, apparently, but I'd never met her.'

'All good with your family?'

Billie nodded. 'Yeah, great. We're reconnecting and I know we'll keep in touch more in the future.'

'Whatever family looks like for each of us, it's important.'

'I agree.'

It seemed the small talk finally got to him like it had been niggling her. 'Billie, tonight-'

'It's okay. Rosie's home. I understand. I don't expect-'

'I hope you do because you're a special part of my life now.'

He stretched an arm around her shoulder and drew her close, running his hand into her hair and pulling her in for a kiss. Billie turned into him and slid her arms around his neck so they could enjoy each other for a while before parting to go their separate ways.

Chapter 14

Next morning, Billie was roused by a little finger gently prodding her through the doona. 'Wake up, Billie, its morning.'

Already conscious but eyes still closed, she smiled and rolled over to see a fully dressed child peering into her face. 'So it is. You always awake this early?'

'Uh huh. Daddy's making breakfast in our new kitchen but we need to collect the eggs first.' Rosie pulled back Billie's doona and tugged her arm. 'C'mon.'

'Did your father tell you to do this?'

'Uh huh.' The child flew out the door.

Billie pulled on trackies and sneakers, shrugging into a puffer coat over the top. On her way through the kitchen, she muttered to Noah at the stove, 'Thanks for the alarm.' She heard his chuckle as she headed for the chook yard.

After breakfast, because Rosie loved getting out around the farm, Noah washed the ute and tidied up the inside before they all piled in.

'We're going for a *ramble*,' Rosie explained, sitting between them on a cushion, obviously having done this many times before.

At one point, Noah let Rosie sit in front of him at the wheel so she could put her hands over his to pretend she was steering across the paddock. The sheep were a winner and brought smiles to her small face. Noah caught and held one for her to feel the wool and explained that one day they would have lambs.

Of course, the question flashed back, 'When?'

'After Christmas, and after summer, when it's autumn and the weather is cooler.'

Rosie wasn't impressed. 'That's a long time away.'

After lunch, Noah suggested a barbeque for dinner. 'With sausages in bread with onion and lots of tomato sauce.'

Billie scoffed. 'That's not a barbeque.'

'It's quick and easy for impatient little girls. Think you could make a cake for afters?'

'I don't know.' Billie glanced down at Rosie, listening intently to the conversation. 'What do you think?'

When she nodded madly, Billie understood that she would be doing all the work with her little *helper* providing the entertainment.

So Noah disappeared to gather wood and get the campfire going again while Billie scouted around in the new kitchen, impressed by the baking wares in a bachelor's kitchen.

'Two decisions,' she said to Rosie. 'What flavour and what shape? Round, square or long?'

'Round.'

'Why?"

'Because you get to cut it in triangles. You can hold it at the big end and start eating it from the little one.'

'Flavour?'

They eyed each other and said together, 'Chocolate.'

Learning how to operate the old black stove and when to feed in the wood to get the right temperature proved a challenge. Rosie cracked in the eggs, helped stir the batter, regularly double-dipping a little finger to taste the mixture.

When the cake was safely in the pan, Billie eyed Rosie and said doubtfully, 'This oven might be too hot but we'll give it a go.'

'What if it burns?' Rosie sounded genuinely concerned, understandable after their joint efforts. Every cook hoped for the perfect cake.

Hands on hips, Billie said, 'We'll just cut those bits off and ice it, or smother it with custard and ice cream. How does that sound?'

Rosie grinned and nodded as she licked the wooden spoon. Twenty five minutes later success was proudly displayed on a cake cooler. Iced and with a thick scattering of nuts and coloured sprinkles.

By dark at the campfire, Noah set a cast iron plate over the hot coals. When their sausages and onions began to sizzle, it smelt amazing. Rugged up seated in camp chairs and eating in their hands didn't allow for much conversation.

With slices of chocolate cake successfully demolished, they sat around the fire, Rosie poking long sticks into the low flames, Noah and Billie simply holding hands and staring into the coals, their thoughts drifting. Being together felt like a family, until Rosie chatted and innocently mentioned something about *Mummy* which brought Billie up with a jolt, remembering her place in Noah's life and that she was really still the outsider here.

Rosie crawled up onto her father's knee and soon fell asleep. He carried her inside and put her to bed. His return promised some quiet time alone together, each sensing need from the other but trying to push back their desire.

'Want to go for a walk?'

'Is this a date?'

He grinned. 'If you want it to be.'

'What about Rosie?'

'Buddy's in the house. If there's a problem he'll bark or come get us.'

'We have to leave the fire?' she laughed. 'It's freezing.'

'It's almost out anyway but I'll keep you warm.'

'Sounds promising.'

They strolled for a while by torchlight then stopped to make out. 'This was a great idea,'

Billie breathed when Noah's hands slid beneath her coat and found bare skin as he gripped her tight against him.

'I couldn't kiss you properly if we were inside. Rosie might wake and walk in.'

'I thought you were the one who liked to live dangerously.'

'Normally I do. Rosie has warmed to you but I'd like to take it slow for her sake. Hand holding or a kiss she can handle but full on passion?' He trailed kisses along her neck, across her cheek and finally claimed her mouth.

'Fair enough,' she chuckled when she could breathe again.

'Besides,' he growled, 'the bedrooms don't have locks on the doors. Yet.'

They lingered, both reluctant to return indoors but the crisp night finally drove them back toward the house. They tiptoed up the steps onto the veranda. Noah's kisses were warm and soft, heating her from the inside until only the two of them existed in the world.

'You're a hard woman to leave.'

'Then stop kissing me because I can't resist kissing you back,' she whispered.

'I best go and douse that campfire.'

Before Billie turned away she watched him descend the steps. The country man who had stolen her heart, sandy hair darker beneath the stars, the body he had shared with her, making her own come alive in the process.

With a sigh, she moved indoors to her room, undressed as quietly as possible by the gentle glow of fairy lights, and was just snuggling under the doona to warm up when she heard puffing behind her. She pushed herself up on an elbow thinking the child was upset only to find her kneeling on the floor, apparently trying to move her mattress.

'I'm sorry,' she whispered, 'did I wake you?'

'No.'

'What are you doing?'

'It's stuck. I can't push it.'

'Where do you want it to be?' Billie wondered if she was missing her father and wanted to go sleep in Noah's room.

'Next to you.'

Their mattresses were only a few feet apart but the child obviously wanted them closer. 'Oh.' So Billie rose to drag it alongside her own. 'Is that okay?'

Rosie nodded and scrambled under her covers again, edging to the side nearest Billie.

Amused and charmed by the incident, Billie bent over and gently kissed the child. 'Night sweetie,' she whispered before resettling herself again too.

Sunday morning, Rosie played outside with Buddy while Noah fetched an old bicycle he found, pumped up its tyres and started teaching her how to ride. The child's laughter and squeals echoed around the homestead, bringing the place alive and endless simple joy to Rosie.

With every hour that passed too quickly, Billie recognised it brought her closer to leaving. At first, she had intended the Wimmera to be an escape and a breather, but meeting Noah Sutton had swiftly changed all that. Even staying for weeks, it had become her home again for that single reason alone.

But after her failed engagement, which brought her to reconnecting with her mother and spending time in a new fledgling relationship, Billie was beginning to understand the issues and commitment needed to make a lasting long term relationship even possible. A genuine partnership in all things. It seemed to be you just did your best, worked at it and above all, talked.

Her sister, Brittany, had apparently waited years to find a good match. She must remember to ask her, in the end, how she knew Ryan was the right one.

Billie herself had jumped in when the first man to show serious interest had grabbed her attention at university. Being young and inexperienced, she had believed herself in love for life, without hesitation living together and eagerly accepting David's marriage proposal. Caught up in the city world of career and ambition, letting it overtake her life. Forgot her roots, ignored her family until knocked out of her comfortable sphere, shaking up everything she had come to know and expect for years.

It still bothered Billie that her relationship with Noah had happened so suddenly and with much stronger emotional force than anything before. She was older now, could see the path of her life to now in a rear view mirror and knew, before her doubts became a problem, she must find a moment to have a conversation with him before she drove away in the morning.

In the afternoon, a stiff wind brought soaking rain, so everyone retreated indoors. Noah lit a fire in the front sitting room. Rosie brought her colouring books and pencils and scribbled for a while. Later, Noah read to her before heading down to the kitchen to make toasties for tea, allowing Billie time with Rosie playing Snap.

Watching the child all weekend brought a growing fondness for Rosie and her antics. An intelligent child with loads of affection to give and be given in return. Despite only occasional visits, father and daughter shared a special bond. Billie reflected all too sadly on her own father and the great loss for both of them that they had not been closer, nor were ever destined to be.

Once Rosie was asleep, an air of the blues hung around Noah when he joined her in the front sitting room before the light of a roaring fire that spread its much needed warmth on the cold night.

'When I put Rosie to bed, I noticed you're all packed.'

She nodded but before she could kick start any discussion, he asked about her plans in the city.

Billie shrugged. 'Take one day at a time. Sort out my rearranged life down there. What about you?'

'In-between farming, finish this homestead I guess.'

It was now or never. 'Any long term plans for the other farmhouse?'

She felt Noah's body grow tense beside her. 'Not really. Still plenty to do getting this house and the property up and running again.'

Whatever the cause, outside the actual death of his parents, Billie believed he was still avoiding some other issue at stake here. 'It still sounds like a problem for you.'

'No. It's in the past. I'm just leaving it there.'

'For now? Or forever?' she challenged.

'Don't push, Billie.'

'I'm sorry, Noah, I don't mean to but there's something still bugging you about that house. When we first met, you told me it takes time to work through personal stuff and that you did it every day. Said you pick up the pieces and move on. I don't understand. What happened over there that you can't do that?'

Noah eased away from her and sat forward staring into the fire, his folded hands between his knees. 'Just has bad memories.'

'I'm just trying to be careful here. I want us to be upfront with each other. I don't want anything between us. Nothing unsaid. No secrets or grief still unresolved that might flare up into a problem later on. I want it all out in the open.'

'Some things take longer than others.'

'Believe me, I understand. I'm still dealing with the trauma Jack caused in our family but I've acknowledged it and I can speak about it. More recently, it was you who helped me realise I was ignoring my engagement breakup and encouraged me to talk. Most liberating thing I ever did.' She gently leaned against him. 'The pain and grief of what we encounter in life might ease but memories can hang around forever. Whatever still has a hold on you, Noah, at least talk about it. No one can force you but, using your own advice and speaking from experience, sharing your deepest feelings will be one of the hardest and best things you ever do.'

Billie could sense from Noah's silence and stiff body language he was emotionally withdrawing from her. The last thing she wanted was to lose him.

Quickly going on, she said, 'Apart from the spark we both felt when we first met, we barely know each other really. I'm learning more about you and your life out here every day. I've met your daughter and I've confided my family troubles to you. But if you're finding it hard to trust me and be honest enough to share your biggest hurt with me this early in our relationship, then maybe until you're comfortable talking about it, we should just promise to keep in touch. I really want that.'

Finally, Billie found a reaction. Noah turned aside to her, strain in his expression, his voice husky. 'I've got used to having you around. I'll miss you.'

Billie struggled to see the agony behind those blue eyes. Her words had hurt him but she also hoped they made him take time and reflect. One of the most decent human beings she had ever met existed behind the strong façade he had created. And the attraction between them was real and firm. But until he could give her more, Billie put a rein on her feelings.

Feeling miserable about their conversation and Noah's denial of any problem about the farmhouse, she felt an obligation to leave him with hope.

'Then maybe I'll come back,' she whispered, spreading an arm around his shoulder and pressing a warm kiss of longing against his cheek because anything more would be her undoing. She rose suddenly. 'I'll leave straight after breakfast.'

Walking out and not turning back cut an ache through her body. Spending time at the shack, getting better acquainted with Noah and meeting Rosie, had all eased back the pace of her once frantic life. She had already worked out that she didn't want to go there again but, if her future was out here in the country, how could she do that if she and Noah were still a work in progress?

Next morning, Billie woke, dressed and stowed her bags in the car. Forced down a few mouthfuls of another of Noah's wonderful country breakfasts and a coffee, forcing smiles for Rosie's benefit before the bitter sweetness of saying goodbye.

'Bye Buddy.' She gave him one final rub.

'Will I see you again?' Rosie frowned.

Billie leant down and scooped her up into a hug. 'Of course,' she said brightly and silently crossed her fingers she would be able to keep that promise.

Noah picked up Rosie and they followed her outside, lingering by the car. The moment should have been happy and sad and wonderful but, instead, it was tense and awkward. But she had said enough last night and there seemed nothing more to add this morning.

'Drive safe,' Noah murmured and with his free arm drew her against him for a generous kiss. For a fleeting moment, they were all in his arms together.

Before tears began rolling, Billie broke away, jumped in behind the wheel and drove away, smiling and waving to cover her private heartache. Not knowing if Noah would make contact or when she might see or hear from him again.

It bothered her that she felt, deep down, they needed to know each other better. The spark and desire between them had been fast and strong, happening quickly. Off the scale. With time, if they were meant to be together, she had to believe it would happen.

Chapter 15

Yesterday's rain became drifting showers so by the time the M8 joined the M1 and she crossed the Yarra River over the Westgate leading her into the city again, Billie's windscreen wipers were pretty much constantly slapping away raindrops.

Had city traffic grown worse since she left or had she simply forgotten its madness? She turned off toward her Docklands apartment, pulled into her underground carpark and took the lift up to her level.

She was scheduled to reappear in her office again tomorrow, already organised compliments of a lengthy phone call with her PA who brought her up to speed at the weekend ready for her return. Seems the office didn't collapse while she was away. A month ago it had been her whole world, her personal and social life lively enough but fitting in around her work commitments. Until that life, as she knew it, collapsed and an unknown future lay ahead.

The lakeside break and attraction to Noah had opened up a fresh outlook and edged her towards thoughts of possible new directions.

Billie knew in her heart returning to her old job would be temporary. After spending time back home in the Wimmera, dissecting where her work could be, working remotely figured high in her options. More people were doing it these days and she intended to be one of them making lifestyle changes.

As she entered her cold modern apartment and dumped her case in the bedroom, Billie pushed out a sigh and finally decided she would respond to David after his countless texts and calls which she had deliberately ignored. He had been like a phantom, constantly appearing on her mobile screen. She knew exactly what he wanted but she needed him to wait. Sweat a bit. And she preferred to do it in person, if for no other reason than to see the look on his face.

As she paced before her balcony windows overlooking Victoria Harbour and the grey dismal day, Billie unblocked him from her phone and tapped out a time for their indoor meeting. He responded immediately.

She used the next hour for unpacking and preparing herself for David's burning question about her little tactic. As a couple, they held no property together and both being in salaried careers, equally shared the rent and expenses. Nothing existed between them anymore, either financial or emotional. Billie needed this final encounter for closure.

Five minutes before the appointed time, she took the lift down to the quiet ground level lounge area in her building and waited. Right on time, she watched David's statement sleek silver Audi slide into a carpark nearby and his hasty strides through the rain. Familiar slicked back hair, designer suit and sunglasses, despite the cloudy day. That arrogant air of privilege to which, unlike her, he had been born.

She was already standing and faced him as he entered.

'Why didn't you answer me?'

Always the need to explain her actions to him. 'I was away and you're no longer in my life.'

'Why did you do it?'

Straight to the point then. 'Because it gave me great pleasure, David.'

'To swap an expensive solitaire diamond for a fake?'

Always about the money. She had suspected as much and expected no less when she slid the substitute ring into the lovely little square royal blue velvet box of the original and had it returned by personal courier. Because it had cost him a small fortune and being paranoid, Billie knew he would have the diamond authenticated as genuine.

'Not normally something I would do. I know it was spiteful but I'm not sorry and, to be honest, I would do it again. The two closest people in my life deceived me. I was beyond cross. Knee jerk reaction, you understand?'

The fury on David's face was also priceless. Where once she had ached for him, love no longer existed in her heart any more. Another man owned that privileged place. This well-groomed pathetic man standing before her she simply despised.

'I suppose you've already sold it?'

'Of course. I'd never keep anything belonging to you. Now you know what betrayal feels like. Stings a bit, huh?' She was gripped with frustration that David should look so deeply offended, as though he hadn't already deceived her, too. 'It fetched a stunning price. But, just so you know, I could never touch a cent of anything that came from you. I donated the funds to charity. Remember, David,' she warned, 'that *you* were unfaithful. Make this difficult and I'll contact my lawyer.'

David's gaze narrowed and he smirked, 'Meredith.'

'Of course, she's the best,' Billie rose and turned to leave.

'You won't do better than a man like me,' David murmured.

Billie paused mid-step. She already had. 'There will never be a better version of you,' she said calmly, 'because you'll never be faithful to any woman. You're no loss to me or any one of them.'

She strode away, back straight, head held high. If he made trouble, Meredith would deal with it but she doubted he would bother. David had already forgotten her while they were still engaged. For now, he had Julia, but would always be scouting for his next conquest.

Up in her apartment again, Billie poured a glass of wine and analysed the wisdom of contacting Julia. To serve one purpose really. They worked together and she preferred to break the ice before she returned to the office tomorrow. Which might prove more irritating than awkward.

Having made the decision, she whipped off a text and waited. As with David, the reply was instant and Julia agreed to the same private meeting place after work, although at that time of day the lounge would be busier. The evening commuter crowd reviewing their day over drinks before spreading out to the suburbs.

Killing time, Billie enjoyed another glass of wine, or two, tucked up on her sofa looking out at the black sky and dismal wet scene across the boat harbour. People scurried beneath umbrellas and trams disgorged passengers.

She was comfortable about the upcoming meeting. While Julia had a part to play in the whole triangle split thing, David was mostly at fault for breaking trust before they were anywhere near the altar. And thank goodness for that, really. Better to learn the truth now. All three had been friends since university. Not anymore.

Downstairs later, Julia finally appeared, feminine and immaculate, and predictably late. Previously, Billie would neither have imagined nor seen her as a threat but she was a gorgeous woman.

'Doing the rounds?' Julia took a seat, searched for a waiter and snapped her fingers to order drinks. 'David said he's already met up with you. Bit nasty about the ring.'

'But necessary.'

'Spit it out. We don't have anything to discuss.'

'We work together, Jules.'

'You're my boss. In the box seat as they say.'

'I would never take-'

'I know. So, just a civil acknowledgement of our changed situation then?'

'End of friendship.'

Julia shrugged. 'Fair enough.' Their drinks arrived, iced water for Billie and a martini. 'David and I were dating before I met you, but we broke it off.'

Billie was actually shocked to realise David and Julia had a history. They had both kept that quiet, never a whisper. Had she known upfront, she might have been more wary. 'I was aware you knew him because you introduced us at the time. I didn't know the two of had been an item.'

'Then you and I became friends, we ran into him together at that university party, remember?' Billie nodded. 'From his first sight of you, he was hooked.'

'Until now,' she murmured.

'I've always been a sucker for smooth operators. They make you feel special. I practically fell into his bed. You proved a bit more of a challenge and I really thought David had met his match. But once a player, always a player, right?'

Billie understood she had no need to warn Julia about David. She was not the soft touch she believed her to be. Beneath the deceptive girlfriend image was a female tease. No point in asking why she had teamed up with David again. As it happened, they were both similar people and welcome to each other. So with Julia's martini swiftly demolished and before she ordered another – which she would be drinking alone - Billie rose, ended the conversation and walked away.

That was enough for one day. She had already arranged a time for a phone chat with Sasha late tomorrow after work and was meeting Melanie for dinner.

Next day, Billie found the routine of fronting up to her glassed-in office on time, dressed and smiling was a far cry from sitting on an old sofa in front of a roaring winter fireplace looking out over a lake, or legs crossed on a floor mattress with her laptop across her knees.

Somehow she endured, met with her bosses, dealt with endless phone calls and emails, and survived her first day high up in the company building. So different to the flat Wimmera plains where she had been in recent weeks.

At the end of the day as the Accountancy Section emptied, she removed her heels and laced on sneakers before heading down to street level and her tram. Shrugging on a raincoat, she jumped on the 35 City Circle, riding it west all the way from the top end of town along La Trobe Street to the end.

From there it was a short convenient walk to her apartment building. Fair enough, it was a decent view along the promenade beside the boat harbour but hardly peaceful and hardly alone.

As Billie entered her apartment, her mobile buzzed in her bag. 'Hi Sasha, thanks for calling. Just wanted to thank you for suggesting the shack as a hideaway for a while. It worked a charm.' In so many unexpected ways.

'You're welcome.' A pause. 'Sounds like you landed in the middle of my brother's drug dealing.'

Billie was relieved Sasha raised the matter but she could hardly have avoided it. 'Worse for you and your family though. How are you holding up?'

She scoffed. 'It's a mess. No one else in the family suspected a thing. We have no idea how he got away with it for so long. The folks are beyond devastated, as you can imagine.'

'Of course. So, what's happening with Mason and Hailey?'

'He was arrested and questioned. Bail was refused so he's cooling his heels in prison until he appears in court. Against Dad's better judgement, he arranged a criminal defence lawyer. Mason has been charged, which probably means many years in prison but they'll appeal for a lighter sentence. Most do about five, at worst nine. He'll be thirty before he gets out but that's still young. We just hope he's learned his lesson. He's always been such a hothead.'

'And Hailey?' Billie prompted.

'She's an accomplice by association although she had nothing to do with the dealing but she's helped police with information. Probably get community service and a fine. Best thing she can do is forget Mason and move on. The girl is so young and mad about him, so who knows?'

Billie briefly touched on other aspects of her stay in the shack and meeting Noah.

'We grew up as neighbours with the Sutton boys,' Sasha said. 'Before Adam was killed. So much tragedy and sadness there.'

'Yeah, I gained that impression.' Billie agreed to keep in touch and they hung up.

She showered and dressed casual for her dinner with Meredith. They were meeting at their favourite restaurant built out over the water. Meredith was running late as usual.

'Sorry, busy day,' she breezed in, all smiles and efficiency.

'Aren't they always?' The sisters hugged.

'Difficult case,' Meredith said taking a seat. 'Thought we might have lost it.'

After they ordered, Billie asked, 'Did you hear about the local drug case back home?'

'Yes! Mason Lowe. Who knew?'

'I talked to Sasha yesterday. Imagine it's been a media nightmare for the family. Had a chat to David and Julia, too. Not together. Getting the hard stuff out of the way.'

Meredith reached out and gripped her hand. 'So, how are you?'

'Making progress. Sorting things out. Met up with Mum and, boy, is she making some changes. Which you know, of course.'

'Great news, right?'

'Not before time but better late than never, I guess. We had lunch with Brittany and Isabelle.'

'Now there's a sweet little bundle.'

'Yeah. I'm determined to get back home more often. She hesitated before continuing. 'I think I might have another reason as well. Not sure. I need your sisterly advice on that or, should I say, counsel!'

'Very funny.' Meredith sat back and took a sip of wine. 'You have my interest.' She upturned her hand and beckoned. 'Okay, give me all the details.'

So Billie did. Over a plate of seafood and a glass of wine looking through a wall of glass to shiny white boats moored in the marina and the city lights reflecting in the harbour.

'Noah was so much older than me,' Meredith said. 'Not sure I even remember him much actually but I've heard he keeps to himself. A loner. That your impression?'

'Maybe. In one way he's strong and capable but in another I believe he's still hurting. Just won't talk about it.'

'Lots happened in his family over the years to cause pain. Two accidents and a divorce. Unless you can push through stuff like that, it can leave scars for life.'

Billie's thoughts exactly and the source of her concerns. She smiled over at her youngest sister. 'How did you get to be so wise?'

'From you, first up. And these days I see a lot of life in a courtroom.'

'No budding romance on the horizon?'

Meredith grinned. 'If there was, he wouldn't be a city boy.'

'Really? I'll keep an eye out for you. Could be tempted to head back to the country myself.'

'Because of Noah?'

Billie shrugged. 'We'll see how it works out.'

'From what you've said, sounds to me like you've already made a serious start.'

'For sure but it's the going on that troubles me.'

'You'll figure it out. You always do.'

Later, the sisters parted. Meredith headed through the city to her tiny worker's cottage in the narrow lane of an inner suburb and Billie strolled back to her nearby waterside apartment.

Reflecting as she nursed a mug of coffee, gazing across the small harbour to the cityscape, Billie identified that doing all this catching up, appointments, phone calls, operating on remote control with her heart no longer in it, she wasn't hurting any more. No longer bugged by regret or disappointment. Her future was gradually falling into place.

She just hoped Noah Sutton was in it. Had a good feeling about the man, if only she could help him in some way to get a grip on his hidden unhappiness.

When her mobile buzzed beside her and the caller ID came up with his name, Billie saw it as fate. A sign that at least he was thinking of her, too, and her heart sped up a little faster before she answered.

'Hey cowboy.'

When he gave that sexy low chuckle and she remembered the grin that went along with it, Billie wished he was sitting beside her and she was in his arms. 'How's the city treating you?'

'Same as always. No surprises but plenty of challenges. Faced off with David and Julia yesterday.'

'That can't have been an easy thing to do.'

'It's done now and I feel free. Spoke to Sasha today and her family's doing it tough. Just got back from dinner with my little sister. How was your day?'

'Missing you,' he admitted softly, 'but Rosie's great company. She'll be here all week and returns to her mother at the weekend.' He paused 'When I drop off Rosie, can I come visit?'

The uncertainty in his voice was adorable but she wondered if he'd given any thought to her suggestion. Reflecting on the people she had confronted and contacted in the last two days so she felt free to pick up the pieces and move on, Billie grew quiet, proud that she had been able to face her demons.

Noah seemed to have accepted his divorce from Michelle, adored Rosie and opened up his heart, if not all of himself, to her. Maybe that was a subject she could tackle when he came down at the weekend. Could go either of two ways and end up in disaster or freedom.

Only problem was, while he was hedging around reality and the truth of his past, whatever that turned out to be, they were both stuck alone and apart. Being with Noah next weekend would definitely ease that deprivation and her entire body hummed with anticipation at the thought.

'I would love to see you.'

Chapter 16

Even though Billie's remaining work week was only three days, they dragged. She found herself watching the clock, leaving on time if not early so she was back in her apartment and snuggled up on the sofa when Noah phoned. Which he did. Without fail.

He always briefly handed the phone over to Rosie who chattered excitedly about what she and her father had done that day. But the child's attention soon faded and she handed the phone back to Noah. Billie loved simply listening when she asked questions because she was always interested in what was happening on the farm. The bonus being his low rumbling tone of voice, the easy way he spoke. She imagined she was in his arms on the sofa in the front sitting room of the homestead in front of the open fire again.

It surprised her that, even though she still felt the weight of an unknown issue between them, the longing ache that scrolled through her body was strong but the moment she picked up the phone, everything else was forgotten.

When Noah arrived on Friday night and Billie caught her first sight of him at her apartment door, all common sense flew out the window. She hadn't dressed to impress. The leggings and overshirt had a purpose. Easy removal. She recognised her need of him. Desire. A force more powerful than free will.

Leaning against the open door, she eyed him up and down. Body packed into denims, warm checked shirt, Akubra pulled low over his face. With an overnight bag in one hand, the thumb of the other hooked through the coat collar slung over his shoulder, here was a man good enough to eat.

Noah's gaze returned the favour, roaming over Billie's bare skin and leading all the way down to the shirt buttons only done up as far as necessary. Not that he seemed in any doubt about the direction of her thoughts. Judging by the sparkle in those eyes trained steadily on her, he caught the message.

He dropped his bag and coat, hauling her hard against him. She removed and tossed his hat behind her into the apartment then they were kissing with longing as though their lives depended on it. They had become lovers recently but Billie's passion meant right at this delicious moment, her heart definitely ruled her head and raced with excitement.

Who could ever explain the logic and chemistry of attraction? It had led Billie to make a poor choice before but this time it didn't only *feel* different. It *was*. In every way. So she trusted her heart and instincts, let her body soak up every need and awareness of this man. Inhaling the earthy outdoor scent and appeal of him, responding to his every touch as he urgently stroked her body in all the right places.

When they finally broke apart, she grinned, Noah looking hopeful and gorgeous in front of her, arms wrapped around her body, still inflamed with desire.

'Did we even say hello?'

Billie chuckled. 'Nope. What shall we do first?'

'I know what I have in mind,' he whispered.

'Think we're on the same page about that.'

He kicked his bag and coat inside, slammed the door and they stumbled more than walked toward the bedroom. They started slow, one touch, one movement at a time. Thank goodness she had dressed light. So much quicker. But damn, shirt studs and belt buckles took forever.

Afterwards, she dozed off and woke much later, their warm bodies snuggled together. Billie rose and pressed a soft kiss to a sleeping Noah's lips, pushing a hand through his thick sandy hair to brush it back off his forehead. He mumbled and stirred but his eyes remained closed. She pulled on a robe and padded into the kitchen where she had stocked up on beer. By the time she returned, he was awake and they shared a bottle.

'Thirsty work,' he murmured.

He was hers all weekend. There was still a conversation to be had before he left but she shoved that thought to the back of her mind and concentrated on making the most of the gorgeous man in her bed and two whole days and nights of the weekend that beckoned.

They sauntered the docklands, took a lazy boat cruise up the Yarra River through the city and lunched on Southbank. Back in the apartment, they made love again and toward evening ate casually at a local fish and chippery beside the water which suited their easy mood just fine.

That night was long and wonderful, Sunday brunch down along the harbour again until they jumped the first tram that stopped nearby and rode it around the city. Hopping off and on as the impulse took them.

By late Sunday when Noah reluctantly talked of leaving, Billie knew she couldn't delay any longer. It was time. She would just have to leap in feet first.

'Thanks for making the trip this weekend. We're good together,' she said, snuggled against him, legs tucked beneath her as they nursed coffee on her apartment sofa.

'We have clicked.' He grinned.

'It's not just in bed. We like the same things, keeping it simple and informal.'

'I sensed it in you from the first time we met. You came from the city but you're a country girl at heart.'

'Hadn't realised until I returned for a while,' Billie agreed. 'I feel comfortable around you, Noah. You're a strong and honest country bloke, and I've already trusted you with my life.' She paused. 'Do you feel that about me?'

'On every level,' he murmured against her hair and pressed warm lips to her forehead. 'Not sure I can imagine my life without you now.'

'When I was back in the Wimmera in the shack and on the farm, we were checking each other out but when it came to the crunch, you didn't hold back. And you haven't this weekend either. It's early days, but do you think about our future?'

'Every single day. In the homestead and out around the paddocks. You never leave my thoughts.'

'Me, too,' she said softly and turned her face up to be kissed. 'Do you think we'll be a part of each other's lives long term?'

'I do, and I'm hoping you want it too.' Hope and question filled his voice.

Billie nodded. 'Do you promise to always be honest with me?'

'Of course.' His brow furrowed. 'Where's this leading?'

She hedged, afraid to say it, knowing she must. 'To the farmhouse.' Noah's pained expression clearly told her he was uncomfortable with her statement. 'I imagine it will be hard for you to share whatever it is you're holding back, but if I'm going to be part of your life, maybe it's important. I'd like to know.'

He pushed out a heavy breath and turned to face her. 'Fair enough.'

'Take your time,' she kissed him softly.

'The false impression everyone has is that our family was normal and functional. Nothing was further from the truth. Every family has its challenges. When you opened up at the shack that day and told me about your parents and siblings soon after we meet, I felt like a fraud. Your situation growing up was even worse than mine and I thought mine was unfortunate enough.

'Expectations.' He turned aside and his gazed fixed across the room. 'Adam being the firstborn son was always the favourite. Wasn't jealous. That's simply how it was. I accepted that. He was keen to be the farmer they wanted him to be. I was just the spare. Even young and still at school, I was glad because I had an interest in flying planes. Before I was old enough to have a licence, I rode my bike for miles across country just so I could hang around at the aerodrome. Pilots and mechanics taught me all they could on the ground.

'There was no pocket money on the farm so as soon as I was old enough and could find any paying jobs in town, I grabbed them. Flying lessons are expensive. For an RPL, Recreational Pilot Licence,' he explained, 'I needed 20 hours. Flight training is available in the Wimmera and they offer a trial instruction flight in a club aircraft to see if you like it. It was the first thing I saved up for. Loved it. Blew me away to be up in that sky.'

Noah looked down at her, beaming. Billie witnessed what she believed was not only relief as he began talking but also glimpses of the happiness that sustained him.

'I was hooked. You can start at 15 but the kicker was needing written consent from the folks. Boy that was a nightmare to navigate. Mum wouldn't agree but Dad finally did and that caused one hell of an argument. They never stopped. When I wasn't needed on the farm, I worked in the local supermarket, for local farmers and tradies, anyone who'd employ me really. As soon as I could afford another lesson, I booked it in.

'I loved flying and that's all I wanted to do. I loved the country life but, at that point, Adam was alive and healthy, no hint of what was to come. Folks were furious and against me but the day I turned 18, I took the flak and joined the Air Force. Every time I came home on leave expecting to be welcomed back into my family, my parents virtually ignored me because they disapproved of my career choice. I felt like an orphan. All my parents' love was for Adam, none spare for me.'

Billie let out a heartfelt moan, wondering if emotional abuse wasn't just as bad as the physical stuff. It left scars. You just couldn't see them.

'It's okay,' he murmured, reassuring her when she felt he needed it more. 'Even young, I understood the blessing to have our grandparents live in the homestead next door. Good or bad days, I raced over there. Our mother was fussy in the house. Didn't like anything out of place, but I always felt welcome and loved in Grandma Rose's kitchen. Grandpa died first so she lived alone for a number of years but they were both gentle loving folk. I've always wondered how they could have a son like my father who was so hard. I look at my own daughter and find it so easy to love her.

'To be honest, I've struggled at the thought of removing that old black stove because it has so many wonderful memories of Granny. But I have them in my mind and heart so I've got a big modern beast on order to replace it,' he grinned, the reflection lightening his mood for a moment.

'Then as if life wasn't bad enough, Adam went out for his usual Saturday night spree with mates and, in the early hours of the morning, wrapped his ute around a tree. The folks were devastated. Their world stopped that night. Through their grief I guess, they blamed me. It was probably easier to transfer their anger onto me because, deep down, they were ashamed and disappointed in their wild oldest son and couldn't accept what had happened. I don't believe they ever did.'

'Where there's anger, there's probably pain underneath.'

'True. Worse still, after my brother died, the folks expected me to leave the Air Force to come home and work the farm. I appreciated they were getting older so I suggested they hire workmen or lease out the property.' He heaved out a sigh. 'One of the most difficult and nasty conversations I've ever had. I understood what they were asking, pleading. The agony on their faces was almost impossible to bear. Now I feel bad because I refused to do as they asked at the time, yet now here I am out of the Air Force and working the place.'

'So all that conflict with your parents is the reason you can't live in the other farmhouse?'

Noah shook his head. 'Half of it. When I met Michelle, they didn't like my choice of wife either.'

'You're kidding!'

'Nope. Even though her parents lived in Melbourne, she chose to live on the farm with my folks for a sense of family. But, she was a city girl, and they considered her out of place on the farm. I know Michelle was unhappy and alone but she stuck it out. Once Rosie came along she focused on being a mother and raising our child, poured all her love into Rosie. She helped my mother around the farm. The folks always had a huge house and produce garden, a big poultry run, sold eggs. But all that didn't seem to matter. They took little interest in their granddaughter. Best reason I can figure out is maybe because Rosie wasn't a boy and we named her for her grandmother.'

'I can appreciate now why it's tough for you to go into that house.'

'Hard to say, but it never felt like a home or a happy place for anyone who lived in it. I never understood why our parents were always bitter and critical. Two very sharp and unhappy people. Life is so precious and you only get one shot at it. Pity to waste it.

'I've often wondered why Adam was drinking so heavily that night. Apparently his alcohol reading was off the charts. And why my father, who was such a careful driver, ended up in a major car accident too that killed him and my mother. Answers I'll never know. Maybe it was simply that split second of inattention they talk about. In both cases, no other vehicle was involved.

'Michelle asked for a divorce and pulled out immediately after the funeral. She couldn't stay in the house a moment longer. Said it gave her the creeps. That was one thing we agreed on. Plus our love had burned out and it was over. From the snatches I hear from Rosie, her mother is much happier now with a new man in her life. Which is important because that reflects on Rosie, too.'

'From what I've seen of you on the farm, you blend into the land. Like it's where you're meant to be.'

'I am. When I first returned, I considered getting work in civil aviation or buying my own small plane but, living alone on the property, back in familiar surroundings, with peace and time to think, I was drawn to the homestead and made the decision to stay and work the place. Ironic, when my parents pleaded with me all my life and, now, here I am. I had the option to sell up and leave but when Rosie visits, she loves it.'

'We can't escape or change the past but we can learn from it. Create our own approach to life.'

'Mine's living in the country. I'd ask you to come and live with me but that would mean giving up your life, friends and career down here. Not sure I even have the right to ask.'

Billie's heart skipped a beat and hoped she hid her excitement. She pulled on a cool expression and said calmly, 'It's a lot to process. I'll think about it. Let's wait and see, huh?'

A while later, when they finally tore themselves away from each other and Noah drove away in his ute, Billie knew it was unfair to keep him waiting. He looked so at home back on the farm but so out of place here in the city. She grinned to herself. Man and ute were part of each other.

After all that had happened in recent months, could she take the leap and make him her future? Life seemed to have steered her into a completely different direction than she would ever have expected. A person knows when a choice is right. Hesitation didn't necessarily mean doubt but merely a lack of courage to take the plunge. At the moment, all her instincts told her that Noah Sutton would be more than worth the jump. Her feelings for him went deep and strong. As incredible as it seemed, she wasn't just falling in love. She already had.

Billie didn't just miss him, when they were apart and she only had his voice on the phone, Billie simply ached for him. Missed Rosie. Rosie loved the farm. So did Billie because of who lived there. All reasons pulling her back.

Plus, as her mother grew older, she wanted to be around for her. Since re-establishing a stronger connection, it was important to nurture it. She'd wised up a lot since her time at the shack and meeting Noah, imagining every aspect of her life and what it could look like.

All developments that called her previous city life into question and why, for so many unbelievable reasons, it would be so simple to move back to the familiar country of her childhood.

As Billie passed the Coach Roadhouse, she was tempted but didn't stop. She'd phone Holly later. Her heart surged with excitement and she was eager to get home. The past two weeks had been a chaotic frenzy. It proved nearly impossible to sound casual in conversation with Noah when he phoned.

The clear blue sky and late winter sunshine enriched the golden wattle bursting into bloom throughout the bush, always the first hint of spring. Finally, she reached the turnoff to the farm and a few kilometres later was turning in at the gate. Would he be at the homestead or out around the property, making her wait?

She'd burned her bridges, tossed it all in and crammed her life into her SUV. Amazing how little a person really needed when everything they wanted was at their destination.

As it happened, Noah's neat backside was seated on the veranda, his feet on the top step, Buddy sitting on his haunches at his side. Where else would man's best friend be? At her approach, both rose as if to attention.

The love in his steady gaze was worth every minute of the four hour drive. 'What do you think you're doing here?' he growled.

'You invited me, remember? Come and live with me, you said? Ring any bells?' Billie took the steps slowly one at a time, ever closer to the man she loved. 'There are places that change us and, for me, coming home to the Wimmera was one of them. Here is where I belong.' She grabbed his sweater and drew him closer so she could whisper in his ear. 'And you belong to me.'

'What if I don't want you?'

'As if!'

Noah's hands gently cupped her face and he claimed her mouth in urgent kisses. 'You're here to stay?'

'Depends on you.'

'That puts a man on the spot. I better figure out quick what I want to say?'

'Fire away.'

'I love you,' he whispered. 'I was hoping to keep you. Forever.'

'That'll do it. Looks like all your dreams just came true. I was thinking we should give it more time but then I figured, why waste any? By the way, the answer's yes. *When you get around to it,*' she emphasised. 'No pressure.'

Billie was proud of him. He was holding back with such strength, pretending this wasn't the best day of his life so far. Of course, seeing her had something to do with that and she was happy to be the reason.

'Rosie will be happy. She told me I should marry you.'

'Sounds like a little girl's princess story to me. You been reading her fairy tales?'

'Rosie's a clever kid and fast becoming wise.'

'She doesn't miss much.'

'Wasn't sure if you were a fan of happy ever after?'

'Depends who's asking.'

'Better not be anyone but me.' As he slung an arm around her shoulder and they turned to go inside, Noah said, 'So, no time frame in mind?'

'Up to you.'

'So, *when I get around to it,*' he repeated with a nudge, 'big or small ceremony?'

'Small. Family and friends.'

'You'll be keeping your name.'

'You know me so well already,' she said with mock surprise.

'Career?'

'Sorted. Start with a local accountant next week.' That little announcement she had been keeping secret both shocked and impressed him.

'Kids?'

'Absolutely. And dogs and probably pet lambs. This homestead will be full of love and laughter and people but,' she warned, 'it might also get rather messy. Hope you're okay with that.'

'Sounds perfect.' He went silent for a moment. 'As you know, I could never live in my parents' house but,' he raised a finger and grinned, 'I would consider maybe letting it out.'

Billie frowned. A stranger next door? Could work with the right person. 'I'm sure you'll find someone.'

'I thought it may suit your mother.'

Billie's heart kicked over and she cried through her smile. 'What a great idea. You've thought of everything.'

She flung her arms around his neck and wrapped her legs around those muscled country hips. No way was she ever letting this man go. He was stuck with her for life. Oh, there was so much to look forward to.

'You sure about living out here?' he challenged.

'What does it look like?' she scoffed.

'Why?'

'Because,' she lowered her voice to husky, 'I love you. I'm going to wake up every morning and you're not going to be anywhere but here with me.'

www.ingramcontent.com/pod-product-compliance
Lightning Source LLC
Chambersburg PA
CBHW072300130726
47910CB00012B/2187